Transfer Hero

Jean —

Classmates are forever. Good ole Maumee High

Jack Michael

Transfer Hero

A Sports Novel

Jack Michael

Library of Congress Control Number: 2011908984
ISBN: Hardcover   978-1-4628-8130-7
                 Softcover   978-1-4628-8129-1
                 Ebook   978-1-4628-8131-4

This book was printed in the United States of America.

To order additional copies of this book, contact:
Xlibris Corporation
1-888-795-4274
www.Xlibris.com
Orders@Xlibris.com
99231

To

My wife, Kathie, the love of my life.
All I do or have done could not have been
accomplished without you.

Chapter 1

Here I am, a junior in high school, and my mother has ordered me to my bedroom. Why are parents still sending their kids to their room? I am sixteen years old, and my mom, why *my* mom, still sends me to my room? It is so darn hot. I have to get outside. Maybe if I explain, she will let me off with a reprimand. No reason not to try.

So it was with a great deal of reluctance and anticipation that sixteen-year-old Mickey Daniels set out for the kitchen to explain to his mother. "Mickey," his mother called, "come in here a minute." As Mickey entered the kitchen tenths of seconds later, his mother said, "My goodness, you startled me. I knew you were fast, but not that fast."

"Well," Mickey started to explain.

"Never mind. If you can give me a reasonable explanation for your actions, you can go on back outside." Mrs. Daniels never liked to keep her son inside when she knew he would be playing ball or enjoying the companionship of any of the boys that she particularly liked. Mickey had slapped the face of a girl, and the mother's call to Mrs. Daniels had really upset her. "Well, Mickey?"

"Mother, I don't know what to say," stammered Mickey.

"All I want is the truth."

"Mother, I . . . I . . . I did it without thinking," Mickey said with a tear welling up in the corner of his eye. "I like Sally, and you know that I would never hit a girl on purpose. You and Dad have taught me better than that. I guess I just saw red too fast for me. I never usually get angry when someone tells

9

me something that I don't like. We have only lived here for a month, and Sally is one of the few people I know. I just don't know what came over me."

"What in the world did Sally say to you that made you slap her face?" A silence followed that Mickey's mother had never confronted before. Her son always answered her. He never lied and was a good son. "Mickey?" Still a silence invaded the kitchen that his anxious mother was unaccustomed to. "Mickey, if you aren't going to explain, you can go back to your room. Your father told me to have you stay there anyway. I called him after Sally's mother called this morning."

"You mean Dad already knows what happened? Gee, Mom, you didn't have to tell him. I would have told him myself."

"Mickey, I didn't know what to do. You have never done anything like this before. You have only been in a fight with one boy since you were twelve years old and now you slap the prettiest girl in the area. Mickey, I just didn't know what to do. Why did you do it?"

"I can't tell you, Mom, but it isn't any big deal. I know she knows why I did it, and if she didn't at the time, she has had time to figure out why. Mom, she doesn't know anything about me or what I like or what I like to do. She doesn't know anything. Man, she just said the wrong thing to me. I guess if we had been among a lot of people, I wouldn't have done it, and if she had been a boy, we would still be out there fighting under the streetlight. How come she waited until this morning to call you? Why didn't she call last night?"

"I don't know, Mickey. All I know is that Sally's mother called this morning, not five minutes after your father left for work and said that Sally had been awake all night, and when her mother questioned her about it, that is when she told her that she had had an argument with the new boy down the street and he had slapped her. I was flabbergasted."

"Aw, gee, Mother. It isn't all that big. I can clear everything up, but I would rather that Dad be here. I know you are not proud of me, Mother, but . . ."

"Mickey, you know better than that. I am proud of you and always will be. You have been a good son. You have never given us any concern except for the time you broke all the windows in that old house."

"Ha-ha! Mom, you remember the craziest things. Pete and I really tore up that old place with our slingshots. How did we know that the only thing they were going to save in that old place was the glass? Anyway, call Dad and see if he can come home for lunch today, okay? I'll try to explain everything to him."

"Can't you tell me? You have always been able to talk things over with me before." Mickey's mother was a little upset that Mickey would not tell her. She had always been a good ear any other time.

"Mother, it isn't anything against you or anything. It is just that this is something that is understood by boys and not girls. You probably wouldn't think that what she said was anything to get upset about. But, gee whiz. I really saw red, Mom. I just got angry. Call Dad and see if he can come home, okay?"

"I'll call, Mickey. You go back to your room, and I'll let you know what he says."

Mickey turned and ambled back to his room. He stared around at the walls that he had been decorating for the past month. They were covered with all kinds of sports figures. His favorite was of Dick Butkus smashing a quarterback trying to pass. What really got Mickey was not the color or the two bodies colliding but the look on the face of the quarterback as he is getting hit.

The sun was shining into the room, and the small portion that filtered between the curtains fell on the face of Bob Hayes on the winner's stand at the Olympic Games after he won the one hundred meters. The sweat of victory was like a light off his sleek forehead, and Mickey knew in his heart that people all over the world were not worried that his skin was black but that he was a winner and that is what counts.

Mickey had worked very hard being a winner while he lived in Moorhead. He knew he had to work twice as hard now that he lived in Fuller. He hated to leave Moorhead. All his friends were there, and he had been the starting shortstop on the Legion team. He was one of two sophomores who had made the team that summer and what happens? His dad gets a once-in-a-lifetime opportunity and has to take it. He had to agree with his dad, though. Becoming the part owner of a sporting goods store beats traveling around the countryside as a salesman, anytime. He has seen his dad more in the last month than he usually sees him in four months.

What will his dad say? It was beginning to bother Mickey. He really respected his dad and knew that he had all the answers when it comes to things like this, and he hoped he would understand how he feels. He gazed at all the old-timers on the wall: Butkus, Hayes, Otto Graham, Paul Brown, Bob Mathias, and Oscar Robertson. They were all winners. Mickey wondered if they had to face things like this when they were young?

Mickey was growing now. He was just under six feet tall. The coach of his baseball team said he was 5 feet 11½ inches. He knew he had to gain weight. The football coach at Moorhead High told him to drink milkshakes every night and eat a lot of potatoes. He loved them both, so that was an easy assignment to carry out. Mickey weighed 166 pounds and that wasn't enough, he knew, but he had already gained five pounds since he came to Fuller. When he was in the eighth grade, he was one of the smallest boys in athletics. He remembered what Coach Dawson had said last month when he and his dad went to tell him of their decision to move to Fuller. I guess Coach Dawson planned on him playing varsity football that year, and he was really upset. He could still hear him . . .

"It seems like no one ever moves in with skills like yours. They always move away. I have seen your son grow up through our school system, and just when you think you have a great athlete on your hands, something goes wrong. The worst part is your family is leaving our community. You will be missed.

Mr. Daniels, your son has the makings of a fine athlete. He has much to learn, but he is more than willing. I remember him coming out to early practices and catching punts from the punters, and I mean he would catch them. They couldn't believe it. They used to have a thing going about who could kick the ball the highest and farthest so Mickey couldn't catch it. He could catch it over the shoulder or on the run, and they would really get angry. After a while, they learned to respect Mickey, and you know, he actually made them better kickers for it. After the season was over, do you remember Granger giving that old ball to Mickey? Well, that is because he got a scholarship to state on his kicking and placekicking."

"Mickey told me that he gave it to him because it was old and they couldn't use it. Mickey still has that on his dresser with the tee the quarterback gave him."

"Well, Mr. Daniels," Coach Dawson said, "I lose my shortstop in the middle of the season and a future all-league halfback. I know that wherever you go you are going to see this fine young man do a great job. Never lose your desire, Mickey, and never lose the one thing that separates you from all the other athletes I have had. That desire to learn as much as you can whether from actual participation or from watching. Good luck, Mickey," Coach Dawson said grasping his hand. Mickey could feel the warmth and strength of the man through that last handshake, and he knew that Coach Dawson meant what he said.

"Good luck in your new venture, Mr. Daniels," he said to Mickey's father as he gave him a final squeeze of the hand and a wink at Mickey. Then, taking his father's hand, he said, "I hope that everything goes your way because you really deserve it. Mickey is an outstanding boy and his next coach is a very lucky man."

Mickey started toward their car because he knew he was going to break into tears. He heard Coach Dawson ask his father if he wanted him to write to his new coach and his father saying, "No, Coach. I think it's best to let Mickey earn his way again as he did here. If he can do the job, they will notice him."

"They will notice him, all right. He is a good one."

Mickey was wondering what Coach Dawson would think of him now. He had actually slapped Sally's face. Actually, he had hardly touched her, but it was the thought behind his actions that was killing him. Mickey sat there and thought about all the things he could be doing with his time rather than being sent to his room. He could be lifting weights in the garage or throwing the ball around outside, or just something other than just sitting there. He had about an hour before he had to confront his father, and he had to do something to take his mind off everything. He used to lie on his bed and memorize all the statistics that were important to each of the players on the wall.

Gosh, seventy-two pictures on his wall. Not any wonder his mother was upset when he told her he was going to put up more. Seventy-two pictures! He counted them again. That picture of Mark Spitz with seven gold medals around his neck. He even won some when he was a teenager. He sure must have had a lot of talent. No, Mickey knew it was more than talent. It was desire and hard work. That was what it was. Hard work, now that is what makes the difference. That is what made you good. Bart Starr said that nothing can really be gained that is helpful without a lot of hard work. He ought to know.

Mickey's eyes scanned the wall and automatically came to the picture his mind kicked into focus when he thought of hard work. Vince Lombardi. Lombardi must have really been great. Boy, would he like to be on a team coached by Vince Lombardi. He knew Coach Dawson was good, but he always quoted Lombardi and knew that Coach respected him. Anyway, the boredom was starting to get to Mickey. Nothing used to bother him. He could be sent to his room, and he would enjoy himself. He played games by himself that took two people and that would occupy him for hours. Now Mickey could only feel the guilt he felt for hitting that pretty little gal. He actually was getting along with her well until the conversation got around to football.

Sally had been filling him in on the team Fuller had for the past season. They were always in the thick of things in almost every sport. Fuller lost only one game last year and that was to cross-river rival Dalton. The Fuller-Dalton game is always the last game of the year, and both teams had gone into the game undefeated. Sally was a reserve cheerleader last year, but they all cheered at the big game. Dalton won 22-8 last year, but she said the game was closer than the final score indicated.

He said a mental, "I'll bet."

Her boyfriend was the star of the team, Billy Brown. He was a junior last year and was the fastest guy on the team. She told Mickey he was all-league and second in scoring. Of course, he was a halfback and the entire backfield was returning. So was Dalton's backfield. In fact, Sally said that Dalton had only three seniors that graduated from last year's starting team and that Fuller lost thirteen.

The conversation got around to Mickey, and she asked him if he was planning on going out for football? He had said sure and that he planned on working hard enough to play in the starting backfield for Fuller this year. Evidently he had taken her by surprise because she began stammering and stuttering and saying, "You'll never do it! You'll never do it!" Mickey didn't know what to say. He looked at Sally, and she came up real close and said, "You'll never be better than Billy Brown." Then she stuck her tongue out at him.

Mickey thought back and the impulse was there again. Slap her. That is the way it happened and that is what he had done. He was sorry he had slapped her, but no one was going to tell him that. They had to show him they were better. He knew there were better players than him, but they had to prove it to him. He would work hard and many hours to overcome the fact that someone was playing ahead of him. The more he thought about Sally's remark, the more it made him angry.

The angrier he got, the easier it was for him to do what he was doing.

Mickey was lying under his bed with the side of it at the line of his chest. He was raising and lowering the side of his bed as if he was lifting weights. He didn't know how long he had been doing it, but he was sweating heavily when his father entered the room.

"What do you think you are doing?" his father shouted. Mickey quickly got out from under the bed and just stood there. "Speak up, Son. What on earth are you doing? You have a full set of weights out in the garage, and here you are in the house, lifting your bed up and down like a rock head."

"Dad, Mother made me to stay in my room, and I guess I just wasn't aware what I was doing."

"Well, come in the kitchen and have some lunch with me while you fill me in on the latest episode of Daniels versus Banning." Mickey had to laugh at his dad. No matter how serious things got, he always tried to make them seem so harmless and that everything isn't so bad. Mickey Daniels versus Sally Banning. He thought about climbing into the ring with her and really giving her something to tell her mother about. Then he laughed at himself again as he liked Sally and his last thought was ridiculous.

"Dad, I am going to take a quick shower before lunch. I'll only be a minute, Mom."

"Don't be long," his dad said. "You know, your mother doesn't like anyone late for a meal, and if I have to come home for lunch to solve a problem, you better be on time."

"Be right there, Dad." Mickey quickly threw off his clothes and stepped into the shower. That was one thing that he did like about the move to Fuller. He had his own bathroom. It wasn't in his room, but it was right next door to his room and none of his mom's or dad's stuff was in there. It was all his. One bad thing, though, he had to keep it clean. Oh, his mother would change the towels and that stuff, but he had to hang up his towel, put the toothpaste away, and things like that, but it was worth it. Mickey loved things of his own, and he actually liked taking care of them.

Mickey quickly showered and changed clothes. He checked his hair in the mirror and scooped up his dirty clothes and headed for the utility room. As he passed through the kitchen, his mother said, "What do you think I am, the laundry lady of the city of Fuller? That is the second set of clean clothes in less than four hours."

"I got the others all sweaty."

"But you were in your room. How did you get all sweaty in there?"

"He was playing Arnold Schwarzenegger," his father said. "Trying to lift his bed to the ceiling."

"Oh, come on, Dad. You know, I was trying to build up my arms."

"Well, use your weights from now on," his mother said.

"I would have, but I had to stay in my room, and you about killed me the last time I lifted in the house."

As Mickey sat down to lunch, he waited for his father to bring up the subject, and he wasn't sure what he was going to say. Mickey never lied to his mother or father, and he knew this wasn't the time to start. He ate the chili his mother set before him and didn't even notice how hot it was. He finished the bowl and asked for another. He was actually almost full, but he knew the more he ate, the heavier he would get. While he waited for his mother to get the second helping, he began to tell his father what had happened. "Dad, I don't know if you are going to understand what I am going to say, but . . ."

"Try me."

"Okay, Dad, but this isn't easy. I am ashamed of what I did, but I am afraid I might do it again if the same thing were to happen. I was thinking about it in my room awhile ago, and I got angry all over again."

"Mickey, just tell me what happened, and let me judge for myself. I know that you must have been provoked, and I just want to know what happened. You don't just go around slapping girls, and I know that, but Mrs. Banning doesn't know that, so just tell me what happened."

Mickey went into the story of the meeting with Sally last night and the talk they had. He explained to his father about the big rivalry that Sally told him about. Then he lowered his head and told his dad what the girl had done to cause him to slap her.

"Dad, I want to apologize to her for what I did, but I am still angry about what she said. She doesn't know me or how good I am or how good I can be. Dad, I want to be the best, and you know better than anyone that I will work hard enough to be in the thick of it. She made her decision on last year's results and didn't even know if I can play football or not."

"Mickey, she probably didn't base her opinion on anything but her loyalty to her boyfriend and her team. You just happened to represent another school, and you aren't her boyfriend."

"Dad, will you go to her house with me and explain that to her mother?"

"Mickey, I'll go with you to the Bannings home, but you are going to do all the talking. Everything you have to gain in school this year may have a bearing on how you handle yourself. Okay?"

"Sure, Dad. Let's go right now."

"Let me finish this piece of pie and then we will give this young lady a visit. Mary? Would you please call the Bannings and make sure they are going to be home?"

"Sure, honey. I knew it couldn't be all that bad. Mickey, I don't see why you couldn't tell me that. I understand all that very well."

"I don't know, Mom. I didn't know if you would react like I would. I can still hear you yelling at me to never hit a girl anytime. I used to get beat up by girls in grade school by not hitting back, and when I did, my third-grade teacher called you on the phone."

"I know, honey, but this is not the same. I guess every boy goes through that and outgrows it."

"Let's go, Son."

"Okay, Dad. I'll go get my shoes on while Mom makes the call."

As Mickey walked toward his bedroom, he thought about facing Sally after last night. He wondered what he would say to her. As he laced on his size 11 shoes, he thought about Sally Banning. Doggone it. She said Billy Brown was better than him and that he would never be better than him. That did it. He was going to show that dumb blonde what a football player is. Billy Brown had all the inside avenues, and he must be really good. He knew that this year he would be wearing the black and gold for the Knights of Fuller High. He liked that. The Fighting Knights of Fuller High. He was going to be the "Black Knight" and knock a few heads together.

As he and his father were climbing into the car together to go to the Bannings, Mickey also thought of the beauty of the girl and how lucky Billy Brown was to have a girl feel that strongly about him. He hadn't had a steady girlfriend in Moorhead, but there were several girls he was interested in. Coach Dawson's daughter was a real nice girl, and pretty, too. Mickey dated her a few times but knew he couldn't make a habit of it, or the guys would have thought he was trying to get in with the coach by dating his daughter. She was the only girl that called him before he left for Fuller.

As the Daniels' convertible was being started, Mr. Daniels asked Mickey, "Where do the Bannings live?"

"Just down the street, about five houses."

"Oh, for crying out loud. Let's walk and get some exercise."

As they were climbing out of the car, Mrs. Daniels stuck her head out of the door and said, "The Bannings are expecting you. Mr. Banning is at work, but they want you to come, anyway."

"We are on the way. Come on, Son, and let's get to know this neighborhood a little better. That is one thing I liked about buying this particular house was the scenery around here. Aren't the trees huge? They must have built this subdivision in the middle of a wooded area. Seems to be a real nice town, Mickey. I think we are going to like it. They say there is a lot of tradition here, and the Fuller-Dalton rivalry is a humdinger. The high school athletic director came in to talk to us today. Seems they are going to get all new uniforms at Fuller this year. If we get the contract, we can make some money. You know, when Clyde Lawson called me to see if I would like to go into business with him, I had all kinds of decisions to make. The biggest was I wanted to have as good a job as I had. The job at the store is great. I meet all kinds of people, and some of the contacts I made previously are helping me at the store. The AD also told me that they sent the football letters out today to the boys interested in playing this year. It has all the pertinent information about the season and the first meeting. I gave him your name and our address, and you will be getting your letter tomorrow."

"That's great, Dad. I am real anxious to get started."

"The AD and the football coach just happen to be the same man. He may stop over tonight to drop off some information about the new materials they need, and it may be a chance for him to meet you."

"Dad, don't say anything to the coach. I want to make the team on my own, and I don't want any favors. I have something to prove to a few people, and I am going to do it. I don't want any help because I have to be certain that the playing I do is because of my ability and not my father's connections. Okay?"

"Right on, Mick. You ought to know me better than that. What you get will be what you earn. No matter the outcome, your mother and I will be very proud."

"Here is her house, Dad. Gosh, I hope I say the right things. I'm scared to death."

"Just be honest, Mickey. That way, you can never go wrong."

Mr. Daniels and Mickey walked up the long walk. It was a big, white two-story house with green shutters and a big screened in porch. There were two large maple trees in the front yard and what looked like a silver maple in the spacious side yard. Mr. Daniels thought he spied a grape arbor in the back, but the house cut off the view as they walked up to the front porch. Mickey was hanging back a little, not from the expected meeting of the Bannings family but from the gigantic size of the house. He had noted that Sally was always neatly dressed, and she was in style, but he never guessed she lived in a house this big.

Mickey had been by this house quite a few times since they moved in but never realized the house was this large. It sat back off the street and that was the deceptive part. The closer he got to the house, the larger it seemed.

Mickey's dad was ringing the bell. The sound of the loud ding-dong brought Mickey out of his trance. What he saw next sent him right back into it. There before him stood the most beautiful woman Mickey had ever laid eyes on. He knew he was standing there with his mouth open. What he didn't know was his father was doing the same thing.

Wow! Mickey thought. Nothing like this is possible. I slapped this beautiful woman's daughter and nothing I say will ever get me off her list. Why couldn't I keep my head? Now I am really in for it. Before Mickey could regain his thoughts, the woman spoke.

"Good afternoon. You must be Mr. Daniels and you must be Mickey."

"Yes . . . yes . . . yes," stammered Mr. Daniels. "My wife called you and said we were coming."

"Yes, I know, Mr. Daniels. I am not in the habit of being able to guess the names of all those that come to the door."

"Yes, yes, of course. Mickey would like to talk to you and your daughter. I hope that she is here."

"She is in the sunroom. She is expecting you and Mickey. I wish I had talked to her a little more thoroughly before I called your wife this morning. I really think the kids could have worked this out on their own."

"Well, let's get them together and get this resolved," said Mr. Daniels. "I have to get back to work. We just moved to Fuller, and I am a part owner in the new sporting goods store down on Main Street, and I haven't really gotten my feet on the ground yet."

"Yes, I understand, Mr. Daniels. Let's go out and join Sally. Come on, Mickey. It is very nice to meet you. Sally's father and I feel we have shirked our duty by not coming to your home and welcoming you to the neighborhood and our city. I know how very difficult it must be to try to make new friends in a strange town."

"We have been pretty busy getting settled, but we figure to get in the swing of things when Mickey gets back into school. I guess most kids don't like to go to school too much, but Mickey is anxious to get started. Actually, he just wants to get into athletics."

"That seems to be the way Sally feels, too. She says Mickey is really hung up on sports. She says she has talked to Mickey several times, and the topic always got around to athletics."

As the three of them entered the sunroom, Sally stood up, and Mickey just stood there with his eyes fixed on Sally Banning. She was so pretty, and he couldn't believe he had slapped her face. Mickey did not speak but walked over close to her and then said in a hushed voice, "Sally, I am so very sorry. I am so ashamed."

He dropped his eyes and turned away from her. He was unable to face her any longer. He knew he had to say something to Sally's mother, but what? What could he say? He had hit her daughter. No man got away with hitting a girl, especially if he wasn't a kid anymore. As Mickey turned to speak, she beat him to the punch.

"Mickey, you are a fine-looking young man."

"Thank . . ."

"Don't interrupt me yet, Mickey. There are a few things I want to say first. I sat here all morning just boiling about the young man down the street that had slapped my daughter. I didn't know what to do or what I should say. Just before your wife called, Mr. Daniels, Sally came to me, and we talked about the situation. She began crying and that is when I thought there was more to the situation than I already knew.

"She began to tell me what happened all over again, and many of the things she mentioned, she hadn't said before. Such as your anxiousness to play for the Fuller High team and how excited you got when she told you she was a cheerleader. She said you almost seemed proud of her. Anyway, she told me what you had said about making the starting backfield. Then she told me what she had said and done. Sticking out her tongue at you, I about died. I wanted to slap her face myself. I want to apologize to you. We raised Sally much better than that, and I guess she reacted the way you did. Anyway, the Bannings do not act like that, do we, Sally?"

Sally looked very sheepish, and with tears in her eyes, she began to speak, "I am very sorry, Mickey. I reacted like a jerk. I am supposed to set the example, not be the example. I guess we both got carried away with our feelings. Mother came down on me pretty hard, and I deserved it and I'm sorry."

There was total silence as the two parents just stared at each other. Mickey was very uncomfortable, but he gathered himself and began to speak, "I don't know what came over me. It is the way I am when I compete. It is hard to explain, but something came over me like only happens to me in a game. I got all fired up and that picture in my mind simply turns red. Sally, I know that I already told you this, but here, you and your mother are apologizing to me, and there is no reason to do so. I was the one at fault, and I am the one that should do the apologizing. I have met just one girl in this town so far, and she is probably the prettiest and what do I do? I slap her face. Then I go to her house to apologize, and she and her mother apologize to me. If you two are any indication of the way this town is, I am really happy we moved here."

As Mickey finished, Mrs. Banning walked over to Mickey and threw her arms around him. She kissed him on the cheek and whispered in his ear, "I hope you beat out Billy Brown this year, too. In more ways than one."

Mickey was overwhelmed. As Mrs. Banning let him go, he stumbled back and looked at his father. He was beaming from ear to ear. He was looking at Sally, and she was doing the same thing. Mickey really felt good. He almost melted when he thought about that beautiful woman throwing her arms around him and squeezing him.

"Well, Son, we better go. I have to get to the store and prepare a price list for Coach Barron, and I want to be prepared."

"Oh," said Sally. "Did you meet Coach Barron, Mickey?"

"No, Sally, I haven't yet. My dad met him at the store, but I guess I am going to get the football letter tomorrow and then I'll meet him soon enough."

"But, Mickey," his father started to say.

"Dad! Let it go at that. Thanks, Mrs. Banning, for being so very nice. Come on, Sally, let's go out to the sidewalk."

As Sally and Mickey walked toward the street, Mickey noticed how pretty her hair was, how blonde and shiny it was in the sun. He noticed how mature she was for a junior in high school. She was about five feet six. Mickey could hold his enthusiasm back no longer.

"Sally, your mother is so nice. Boy, she is really pretty. I didn't know what to say while she was standing there in the doorway. Boy, Sally, I'm glad that is all over. I was worried all morning. I'm really sorry, Sally. If I ever lay a hand on you again, I hope a Mack truck runs over me."

"Oh, Mickey, don't be silly. You did what anyone else would have done. I feel like a dum-dum. Can you imagine a sixteen-year-old girl sticking her tongue out because she can't think of anything to say? I hope that is the last stupid thing I do. Did you know that after I told my mother what actually did happen, she hit me on the rear with her hairbrush?"

"Oh, you're kidding! Your mother wouldn't do that, would she?"

"She did. She was more angry at my letting her call your mother than she was about me sticking my tongue out. She was going to make me come down to your house and apologize to you and your family when your mother called her."

"That is really funny. I slap a girl in the face and the girl's mother thinks it is her daughter's fault. Now, that is funny."

"You should have seen her right after I told her what happened early this morning. She would have scratched your eyes out. She was really angry with you."

"Well, I'm glad everything is okay, now. Your mother is so nice. I would hate to have her angry with me. I hope I can meet your dad sometime soon."

"Oh, you'll get to meet him. He is the president of the Boosters Club this year, and he just loves football. He thinks Billy Brown is the greatest."

"What do you think, Sally?"

"Oh, he is pretty nice. He sure is big. He is about three inches taller than you and really has a good build. You know, what I mean. The swimming coach wanted him to be a swimmer but he likes basketball."

"Do they have a pool in the high school?"

"Yep, it is one of the best in the state. The team is good, too."

"I have only seen one swimming meet in my life."

"Are you coming, Son, or are you going to stay? I told them I would be back at the store by one and that only gives me about fifteen minutes to keep from being a fibber."

"I'm coming, Dad. I'll see you later, Sally, and thanks for being as kind as you are. Thanks, again, Mrs. Banning," he yelled to Mrs. Banning, who was standing in the open screen door of the front porch.

"Come and visit again, Mickey, under more pleasant circumstances," Mrs. Banning yelled. "Bring your wife down for a visit, Bob, and meet my husband."

"We'll do that, Nancy. Thanks, again," Mickey's dad said.

Mickey and Mr. Daniels began the walk home, and all sorts of things were going through his head. Gee, he didn't really have to apologize after all. Mrs. Banning had made it so very easy. She had made him actually feel that she really did forgive him and that some of the blame was Sally's. He never dreamed that all this could happen.

Then, Mrs. Banning throwing her arms around him and whispering in his ear. That really got to him. Maybe someday Sally will do that. If she ever gets to be as pretty as her mother, that will be something. Then his dad calls her Nancy, and she calls him Bob like they are old pals. He never expected that. Mickey thought that Mrs. Banning was going to tear into him and his dad. Mickey began to chuckle.

"What's so amusing, Mickey?"

"Oh, I was just laughing about what happened and how it happened. What I was really laughing about was the Nancy and Bob farewell."

"Oh, cut it out, Mickey. She insisted on not calling each other mister and missus, and I agreed. There is nothing wrong with that."

"I didn't say there was, Dad. I just mean that I didn't expect it. She sure is a pretty woman, isn't she?"

"She sure is, Mickey. Her daughter is a knockout, too. She seems to have a lot of poise for a young girl. She couldn't keep her eyes off you. I actually think that she likes you a little more than she is willing to admit."

"Come on, Dad. You can tell all that just from the way she looks? Besides, Billy Brown is her boyfriend, and I am going to beat him out of his job on the football team this year."

"That is going to be quite a job, Mickey. From what I have heard from the people here since we moved to Fuller, he is really something. They are starting to get football fever already, and all they talk about is Billy Brown and the way the Black Knights are going to smash the Dalton Red Raiders."

"Dad, there isn't anything more in life I want right now than to be in the starting lineup when the season starts and to beat Dalton. I mean the starting backfield, too! Hey, do you want to play catch when you get home tonight?"

"If I'm not too tired, Mickey, I'll be glad to. Let's tell your mother how things came out and then I have to get back downtown."

Several hours had passed and Mickey had spent them kicking the ball in the side yard. He felt he was lucky to have a big side yard. He used his tee and placekicked at the makeshift goalposts he had put up between two trees. He measured it and it was five inches too high, but he figured that would help him. He decided to leave it like that, and if a ball hit the crossbar, it would be good. He would kick from twenty yards out. He visualized the kickers on his wall, Lou Groza and the others, and they all had their own style.

Mickey would kick the ball off the tee and sprint after it on the other side and kick a heel print in the ground and place the ball there and kick it back. That way, he was practicing with and without a tee. He remembered his dad telling him about the old days and using the dropkick. That was hard. He would try it, he thought. He kicked the ball off the tee, and the ball sailed high over the bar and dead center. It rolled toward the street. Mickey saw a car coming, so he sprinted after it as fast as he could to prevent them from crushing it. He got there just in time to prevent it from rolling over the curb. Mickey scooped it up in one fluid motion and headed back toward the bar. Instinctively, he dropped the ball to the ground and tried the dropkick. The ball hit the ground at the same time he was kicking it. The ball soared into the air. It went about fifteen feet above and beyond the bar. Mickey couldn't believe it. He started to pace it off. Wow, a thirty-two-yard field goal. It would have been good from even farther.

Mickey was resetting the ball on the tee when he saw two boys heading his way. He saw the car parked at the curb that had almost been the end of his old football. He looked the two boys over and noticed how nice and clean-cut they looked and how well-muscled they were. They both were wearing T-shirts that had FHS FOOTBALL printed on the front . . .

"Hi," the biggest of the two said. "Are you from around here?"

"Hi. Yes, we moved into town last month. I live right there in the brick house. My name is Mickey Daniels."

"Glad to meet you," the boy said. "My name is Randy Mason. I live in the next street over but down about five blocks. Man, that was some kick you just made."

"Ha-ha! That was just lucky. To be honest, it was the first time I have ever tried a dropkick with my football shoes on. I must have hit it just right. My grandfather used to kick that way all the time when he was in school."

"That is as far as any placekick I've seen Billy Brown kick," the other boy said. "I'm Chad Anderson, Mickey. Glad to meet you."

"Hi, Chad. You guys play on the high school team?"

"Yeah," Randy said. "We both got the letter of 'pain' today, and we both went down to Red's and got a haircut."

"The letter of 'pain'? What is that?" Mickey asked.

Both boys laughed and slapped each other on the shoulder. "He doesn't know what the letter of 'pain' is."

"Boy, what a way to be introduced to the city of Fuller."

"Barron's beauties of the early practices."

"Two-a-days for three weeks."

"*Aaarrrgggghhh!*"

Both boys were throwing comments back and forth, and Mickey was eating it up. He finally got the message, and they all were having a good laugh. Mickey actually had tears in his eyes as he watched Randy roll around on the ground in fake agony.

"Mickey," Chad said. "Are you going out for the team this year?"

"I sure am, Chad. I hope that I can make the team. I hear you guys are really good and had a great season last year."

"We had a real good team last year," Chad said. There seemed to be a little hesitancy in his speech as he continued. "We went into our last game undefeated with Dalton, and they beat us 22-8. The score was no real indication of the actual game. The score was 14-8 with about three minutes to go, and Coach Barron decided to go for it on fourth and one on our own 19. I dropped the ball handing off to Billy Brown, and they went in to score another TD just before the end of the game."

"That's not true, Chad, and you know it," Randy said. "Mickey, this is the finest quarterback around, and he always takes the blame for everything. He didn't drop the ball at all. The films show it very clearly. The only one who says you dropped the ball is Billy Brown. Mickey, we really did have a good team. We had thirteen guys graduate from the starting twenty-two positions. Three guys played both ways, and they were all juniors. It's Dalton that is going to have the great team. They only lost three guys, and I think the only reason they played was they were the tri-captains. Shaw was a pretty good linebacker, but he can be replaced."

"You know, I met Sally Banning, and she told me many of the same things. She told me the same thing about the score being no indication of the game, and I thought it was a lot of hot air. I guess I will have to apologize to her again."

"Again?" Chad said. "What happened? How did you meet her? Do you know she is Billy Brown's girl?"

"Yes, I know all that. She just lives down the street, and we were talking last night. Well, anyway, that is when she told me her boyfriend was Billy Brown and how great your team was and what a great rivalry you have with Dalton."

"Well, you better stay away from Sally," Randy said. "Billy gets really angry if anyone even talks to her."

"I'm not scared of any Billy Brown, and he certainly isn't going to tell me who I can talk to. If Sally doesn't want to talk to me, she will tell me so. Gee, I hope there aren't going to be any hard feelings between us."

"Gee, no," said Chad. "We just thought we would let you know about Billy Brown."

"Thanks, Chad. Come on, do you want to throw the ball around a few times?"

"Sure, give me the ball and take off."

Mickey took off and ran along the side of the yard. Chad lofted a long spiral, and it hit Mickey in full stride. Mickey pulled the ball in and came to a halt. He turned and saw Randy cutting across the yard and waving his arms. Randy was about six feet three and 220 pounds, and Mickey noticed he moved very smoothly. Suddenly, he cut in a different direction, and Mickey let the ball go. Randy hauled it in, stumbled, and fell forward. He did a neat forward roll and was on his feet waving the ball in the air like he had just scored the winning touchdown in the Super Bowl. He bowed and then went into a little dance and slammed the ball down hard.

Mickey cracked up. That Randy is a real nut. As Randy was throwing the ball to Chad, he noticed how Chad handled himself. Chad looked about the same size as Mickey, maybe an inch taller at six feet. Randy had thrown the ball over Chad's head, and he leaped high, tipped the ball, and, in three or four different moves, caught the ball. Good hands, Mickey thought. They both seem to be natural athletes.

"Go," yelled Chad. Mickey took off in a sprint. He faked left and moved to his right. Chad fired the ball in front of him and a little high. He jumped at the right time, and the ball still seemed too far for him to grab. He threw up his left hand, and the ball smacked right into it. As a natural motion, one which was natural to a baseball player, he snapped his left hand down to his chest area, where he met the ball with his right hand. He hung onto the ball for dear life as his body turned and twisted to the ground. He hung onto the ball as his body crashed to the ground. He rolled onto his back and then on to his feet. Both boys were just staring at him.

Mickey walked over to them and asked, "What's the matter?"

"Did you play football where you used to live?" Randy asked.

"I played reserve ball. It was a big town, and they had a rule that all ninth and tenth graders had to play reserve ball unless they were unbelievably good."

"What did you play?" Chad asked, "End?"

"No, I was a halfback. There isn't enough action at end for me."

"You catch the ball like an end," Chad said.

"Ha-ha! Both you guys catch the ball well, too. Come on in the house and get some lemonade. I want you to meet my mother. She thinks the only one I know around here is Sally Banning."

"Gee, we'd like to, but . . ." Randy started to say.

"Oh, come on. Take five more minutes and meet someone you will never forget."

As they headed for the house, they jabbered back and forth about the soon-to-be-started early fall football practice, which was usually painful. No wonder they called the letter from Coach Barron the "letter of pain." He remembered the awful early practices at Moorhead. He thought it funny they hadn't asked him where he had moved from. Maybe that was an indication that they really didn't care, that they were from the best town and the rest didn't interest them.

As the three boys entered the back door, Mrs. Daniels was walking toward them with three giant glasses of lemonade. The boys were astounded.

"Hi, boys. I thought you might enjoy a glass of lemonade to quench your thirst."

The three boys laughed long and hard, and Mickey told her, "Mom, you never cease to amaze me. I just asked them if they would like a glass of lemonade, and here you are, bringing it out. Do all mothers have mental telepathy?"

"I know mine does. Every time I am about to do something wrong, my mother is on the scene." Randy laughed. "Hi, Mrs. Daniels. I'm Randy Mason. This is Chad Anderson. We jus bin wingin' the ole pigskin about in the side yard."

"Yes, I know. I was watching you. You have a very fine passing arm, young man," she said to Chad. "And the agility of a cat. You must be the quarterback, whereas you, Randy, must be a frustrated fullback who has been placed on the line to knock people down so other people can get the glory."

All three boys just sat there and looked befuddled. They were taken back by Mickey's mother.

"Mother, you are either going to embarrass them or make them angry."

"No," Randy said. "You weren't kidding, Mickey, when you said she was great. You read right through us and through our coach, too. How did you know that I was a lineman and wanted to be a back? How did you know Chad was the quarterback? Gee, that is fantastic, Mrs. Daniels. You really amaze me. I don't think half the people in town that have seen us play could tell us what you just finished telling us. How do you do it?"

"Well, it isn't all that hard. The way Chad throws the ball and the way he motioned you two around indicated he is used to running the show. And Randy, that is the neatest dance I have seen in a long time."

They all laughed heartily at her comments. "Besides," she continued, "most boys your size are linemen in high school. Your show of emotion showed me that you don't get to do that very often."

"That's very good," Randy said. "You ought to be a detective or something. Say when Dalton is ready to call their plays, we can have a hotline to you, and you can tell us what they are going to do."

"You boys will do just fine without me this year. Why, if you play like you did in the side yard a while ago, you won't lose a game."

"That's our goal, Mrs. Daniels," Chad said. "We want to win them all. We won eight straight games last year, and we didn't even break into the top twenty teams in the state. We are a small team, so is Dalton, and Coach Barron says that is the reason. He says we have a better chance to make the listings this year because we did have a good year last year. Dalton and Fuller should go into the last game undefeated again this year. Dalton has almost everyone back, and they will be really tough. We lost a lot and have two new teams on our schedule this year, and they are good football schools. If we can beat them, it will help us get rated. Say, Mrs. Daniels, did Mickey get his letter from Coach Barron today?"

"No he didn't, but . . ."

"Never mind, Mother. Dad said he was sending it out and that I would be getting it tomorrow."

"The 'letter of pain,' Mrs. Daniels," Randy said. "Better start feeding him plenty of vitamin C and salt tablets. He is going to need them."

"We went through all that last year with Mickey. He was growing a lot, and we were really worried. The doctor almost told him to lay off. He grew six inches in almost seven months. We could hardly believe it."

"Well, we better get going," Chad said. "It was nice meeting you, Mrs. Daniels. And thank you for the lemonade."

"It sure was, Mrs. Daniels," Randy filled in. "Very educational, too. Mickey, I know that you will have fun on the team this year and welcome to Fuller. I know that you will like the town and the people, too."

"Yeah, Mick," Chad said. "It was nice meeting you, and I look forward to playing ball with you. As soon as you get 'the letter of pain,' you will officially be a Black Knight."

"Bye, guys, see you soon. If you want to throw the ball around, stop again, and we can work out a little."

"Bye. See ya. Be good."

After all the exchanges of good-byes were over, Mrs. Daniels turned and gave Mickey a big hug. "They are such nice boys. I hope they all are like them. Wouldn't it be nice to have all your friends be like Chad and Randy?"

"That would be great, Mother. I think I will go out and lift weights until Dad gets home, okay?"

"That will be fine, Son. Be careful. You know, what your father said about lifting weights alone?"

"I know what the maximums and minimums are, Mother, and I am not going to do anything that will strain a muscle. I just want to be ready for Coach Barron's program and the great Billy Brown."

Mickey headed out to the spacious garage. It was actually a two-car garage, but the Daniels only had one car. Mickey had his weight bench set up in front with his ping-pong table set up in the other half. It was the kind of table that could be set up with half of it flat and half upright. He could play by himself with the upright half rebounding every hit. Mickey picked up the paddle and ball and began to volley it. Before he knew it, he was really going at it.

Mickey was challenging his right hand to his left. He knew that would help his coordination as well as hand and eye. As time passed, Mickey moved back and hit the ball harder. The thought kept coming to him that if he kept this up, he would go out of his mind. He loved to win and the table rebounding the ball never missed a shot.

Mickey had been playing table tennis for about twenty minutes so he decided to lift a few weights. It wasn't a matter of getting so strong that he would be muscle-bound, but he did remember what Coach Dawson said at Moorhead. You need the strength in your arms for a very good reason. No matter how hard you are tackled or how hard they try to get the ball out of your arms, you never fumble. Coach Dawson hated that word. He didn't agree with everything Bo Schembeckler did at Michigan, but he says that a fumble is a weakness and that weaknesses ruin ball teams. Mickey prided himself on the strength he had in his arms. He never lifted weights before and had only been doing so for about two months. Still he had what his coach said, "The strongest throwing arm on the team." Mickey didn't want to fumble. A newcomer would be lost in the shuffle if he couldn't hang onto the ball.

Mickey put 105 pounds on the bar and reclined on the bench. All he wanted to do was use this weight and keep repeating the lift. More weight wasn't as important as how many times he could lift it. Besides, if he got a weight on the bar, he couldn't lift after he got it off the rack, he might hurt himself.

Mickey lifted and thought about the school year ahead. What was in store for him? He knew one thing for sure. He was going to give that Billy Brown a run for his money on the football field. Sally had said they have a pool and a swim team. He loved to swim. Maybe he could go on rec nights and swim. He did pretty well at the Y camps. Coach Blank at the camp was impressed that Mickey was so good without any formal training. He told him he ought to be a swimmer, but with no pool in town, he hadn't given it another thought.

Mickey got up and put another ten pounds on each end of the bar and decided to test his endurance. Could he lift this ten times? He settled under the bar and thought about what Chad had said about messing around with Billy Brown's girl. He didn't know why he was so irritated about why Billy Brown had a girl or that other people were trying to help him out by warning him. I guess, Mickey thought, the big thing is that Billy Brown's girl is Sally Banning. What should he expect? Sally had to be one of the prettiest girls in the whole town and Billy was the talk of the town.

As Mickey was straining under number nine, his father walked into the garage. Mickey took a deep breath and tried number ten. His body quivered and shook, but he finally got it up. He let the bar and weights fall back on the Y-shaped rack and let out a big gasp.

"Dad, I'm glad you came in when you did. If you hadn't been there, I couldn't have tried that last lift and that has been my goal for over a month."

"I'm glad to hear you have common sense about your lifting, Son. I don't want you doing anything in here by yourself that would hurt you."

"I know that, Dad. That is why I am glad you came in when you did. Is it time for supper?"

"I don't know yet. I pulled into the drive and, when I was walking up to the house, I heard you in here working out and wondered how you were doing. How much do you have on the bar?"

"One hundred and twenty-five pounds. That was my goal for a long time now. To lift 125 pounds ten times. Do you think it is impossible to lift my own weight ten times?"

"Well, no, Son, but for you it could become a major project. You are gaining weight all the time."

"Well, I weigh 166 now. At least I think that is what it is, and my goal is 165 ten times. I guess I better stick at that weight if I am going to get fat."

"That is a fine goal, Son. In fact, that ought to give you something to shoot for the coming year. Come on inside and get cleaned up. Your mother will have supper ready soon, and I am hungrier than a bear."

"Okay, Dad. I'll clean things up in here, and I'll be right in."

Mickey really enjoyed his dad. He always seemed to have a genuine interest in him and concern for how he was doing. Gee, he thought, he forgot to ask his dad if Coach Barron was still coming over after supper tonight. Mickey actually hoped his dad had taken care of things at the store so that the coach wouldn't have to make a special trip to the house. He may think that is just a way for his dad to get interested in his son. It is Saturday, the 16th of August, and Mickey knew that the practices were going to start the following Monday. He knew that if the coach had any interest at all in him as a new ballplayer, he would have to bring the letter tonight. He would get it too late Monday to do him any good.

Hey, he had better get hustling. And clean up for dinner. No sense getting his mother upset after she had been in such a good mood earlier.

Chapter 2

Mickey was lying on the floor, reading the sports section of the *Daily News,* and his father had the front section while his mother was finishing the dishes. The news on the TV was about the flood on the Ohio River. Mickey was wondering if they ever had floods on the Ross River, which is the river that separates Fuller and Dalton, when the doorbell came on.

Mr. Daniels answered the door. Then Mickey heard a deep and aggressive voice say, "I'm not too early, am I?"

Mickey's father answered, "No, you're too late. We are all done eating."

The two men laughed and entered the living room. Mickey jumped to his feet as his father spoke.

"Mickey, I want you to meet Coach Barron. He is the football coach and athletic director at Fuller High. This is my son, Mickey."

"I'm very glad to me you, sir. I have heard a lot about you."

"It is my pleasure," said Coach Barron. "I brought you a better ball to practice with. The boys said you have a real punkin, your throwing and kicking around."

Mickey was taken aback. He didn't know what to say. He stammered, "I . . . I . . . who, where did you hear about me?"

"Well, Randy Mason and Chad Anderson stopped by the house this afternoon and said they met this new kid that had hands like Jerry Rice. They proceeded to tell me about this long dropkick you made."

"Ha-ha! Those guys are nuts. They are really great guys. We had a pretty good time. But they are a little over their heads when they say I can catch like Jerry Rice."

Mickey immediately thought about the picture on his wall of Jerry Rice. The ball was on his fingertips and his body at a forty-five-degree angle leaning out of bounds and his toes just inside the sideline stripe. No one can catch like that man. He used to slide in that position for five yards until Montana laid the ball into his hands.

Mickey's dad broke the silence. "It isn't because he hasn't been offered a new ball. The kicker at his old high school gave it to him a few years ago. He has had it since the seventh grade, and he won't part with it. We bought him a new ball two years ago, and it is still in the box in his room."

"Well, Son," Coach Barron said, "you have to learn to catch a new hard ball if you are going to play with us. Those soft punkins are pretty easy to catch."

"Yes, I know. I can catch a ball, and I always use a new one except here at home. I guess I had better start using the new one, eh?"

"You sure should, Mickey. Here is a copy of the letter that all prospective football players at Fuller get telling them what I expect and the date and times to report. Also, here is a playbook that we used last year, and I thought you might like to look it over. Don't lose the letter, the playbook, or the ball, okay?"

"Thank you very much, sir. I'll take care of all three, especially the letter. I have been waiting for this since we moved here a month ago." With that, Mickey excused himself and headed for his room.

"By the way," Coach Barron called after Mickey, "what position do you, or should I say, did you play last year?"

"I played halfback, sir."

"Oh," said Coach Barron, a little halfheartedly.

Mickey continued to his room, where he sat on his bed and began to read "the letter of pain."

Dear Football Candidate,

You have been, or are going to be, part of the finest football program in the state. The Fuller coaching staff is anxiously awaiting Monday, the 18th of August. Set that date aside. That is the first day of football for the coming season. You are to be at the high school by 8:30 a.m. The doctor will be there waiting for you. *No one is to be late.*

Following the physical, equipment will be given to all seniors first, then juniors, etc. Following equipment checkout, all ballplayers will fill out a personal information form. You will then be dismissed and will return to the high school by 2:30 p.m. for the first practice. For those that don't know what to expect, you will start a heavy conditioning program. We will be the finest conditioned team in the state, and we will always look that way, too. The first several practices will be without equipment with the exception of helmet and shoes.

You must provide your own shoes, and we suggest they be broken in. There will be no lost practice time due to blisters. Blisters are for the sissies at Dalton.

You are to bring your parents' permission form on Monday, and anyone reporting with hair that sticks out the bottom of his helmet or the ear holes will run a lap for every hair we see.

Training rules are in effect, and you all know that means alcohol, liquor, tobacco, drugs, and late hours. Late hours are 11:00 p.m. on weekdays and twelve thirty on weekends.

Our goal is to go all the way this year, be rated, win league, and make the playoffs. Anything that gets in the way of those goals will be quickly eliminated.

Again, welcome to the Fuller High School football team. You are now a Black Knight. Act like one.

Sincerely for football.

Enclosed is our schedule this year. Learn it and become familiar with each team. Each one is a personal goal of each member of this team. Keep your grades up.

Mickey loved what he read. Coach Barron must really be a fine coach. There won't be any fooling around at his practices, you can bet on that. Just looking at Coach Barron, you know that he wants clean-cut kids to play ball for him. Now I see what Randy and Chad meant by getting a haircut after receiving the "letter of pain." Mickey also liked the thought of no pads for several practices. He knew that he was in shape, and that he could take it, but he was going to have a chance to look everyone over before he had to get into the heat of battle. Mickey wondered whether these guys were as good as the Moorhead boys? Were they the same kind of deadly hitter? Mickey could remember the number of times he had his "chimes" rung last year. The Moorhead boys liked to hit and so did the teams they played.

Mickey took the enclosed sheet of paper with the schedule on it and checked out who they played. There it was black on white. That was the object of the year. This was the schedule that they all had been waiting to see.

Fuller Football

September 8	Torrence	Home
September 15	Bradon	Away*
September 22	Avon	Home*
September 29	Bluffton	Away
October 6	Kensington	Home*
October 13	Howard	Away*
October 20	Cade City	Away*
October 27	Melvindale	Home*
November 3	Dalton	Home*

8-22: Need we say more?

Mickey awoke Sunday morning just in time to smell one of his favorite aromas, the smell of bacon and eggs. Usually, he would have a cold cereal and several pieces of toast and maybe cocoa, but Sundays were rather special to Mrs. Daniels. She always liked to have bacon and eggs with as much orange juice as her boys could drink. Mickey quickly got up and jumped in the shower. He was really happy this morning. He was so happy; he decided to take his mother to church. She had been after him ever since they moved in to go to church, but he always came back with the excuse that he would start going after school started. Even his parents had not been there yet. Mickey knew that his dad would beg off because he liked to relax on Sunday. Mickey guessed his dad was home so little during the week when he was a salesman that he didn't like to go anywhere when he had a chance to stay home.

Mickey toweled and padded his way into the kitchen wrapped only in towel. He sneaked up on his mother, and just as he was going to scare her, she said, "Do you want two eggs or three?"

Mickey was surprised and said, "How did you know I was there? You didn't see me."

"Oh, Mickey, your mother knows everything."

"I'm beginning to believe it. You are really something, Mom, you know that?"

"I get by. Besides, you stopped singing and humming, and I knew you must be up to something. Then I saw your reflection in the kitchen window."

"Ha-ha! You really ought to be a detective. Say, Mom. Do you want to go to church with me this morning? I decided I better go before football season starts. I may need all the help I can get."

"Why? Sure, Mickey. I'll fix your father's breakfast and then I'll go change."

"Good. The service starts at eleven and that will give us forty-five minutes."

Mickey went back to his bedroom and started laying out his clothes. He put on a clean T-shirt and undershorts and then slipped his slippers on. It may be August but this floor is really cool in the mornings, thought Mickey. That may be a big help for the morning sessions of two-a-days. If it is cool early, they won't sweat to death when they are doing their drills.

Funny, thought Mickey, how he always drifted back to thinking about the up-and-coming football season. Everything he does seems to lead up to his thinking of football. His mother had just called him to breakfast, so he went in and devoured three eggs, six pieces of toast, and three glasses of orange juice. His mother sure knows how to cook. He ought to gain a little weight from all the food he has been eating lately. It is a good thing his mother had remembered about his milk shake last night. He was already in bed when she brought it in. Mickey ought to get her to make them all the time because she makes them so much better than he does. Out of curiosity, he drifted into his bathroom and climbed on his own special scale. He had the letters "GOAL 185" on the top. He looked down. He couldn't believe it. He got off and climbed back on. It read the same thing, 173. Gee, he had weighed just 166 four days ago. It just didn't seem possible. He looked at himself in the mirror. He couldn't see any difference. He did seem to be filling out a little more, but gee whiz, seven pounds in four days. Mickey was really excited about the added weight.

He looked in the mirror, again. He knew he didn't have to get a haircut because his light brown, sort of blondish, hair was not longer than an inch and a half anywhere on his head. He never did like long hair. He never had anything against it, but he couldn't see all that hanging from his head if he didn't need it. Besides, it always seems to be getting in the face of those guys that let it grow. Mickey made sure the part was okay and then went back to his room to get dressed. He put his favorite sport coat on and double-checked the shine on his shoes. Better touch them up a little. When he had finished, he went into the living room, where his dad was reading the sports page.

"Say, Mickey. It says here the Dalton Red Raiders are picked to be the league champions with Fuller and Melvindale picked to finish in a tie for second."

"Well, that is better for us because we have something to shoot for, and Dalton has to stay on top. When we get through with them, they will shoot the sports writers."

Mrs. Daniels came into the living room, and Mickey let out a whistle, took his mother's arm, and headed for the door. "See you after church, Dad. I have a date with the loveliest lady in Fuller."

"You sure do. See you later."

Mickey helped his mother into the car and ran around to the other side. He didn't normally get to drive the car, but that was one way his mother used to get him to go to church. Mickey started the car and backed out of the driveway.

Mickey and his mother drove in silence as they worked their way toward the cute little Presbyterian Church down the street. He remembered seeing it as he walked around after moving to Fuller. It wasn't more than seven or eight blocks away. He spied a parking space about three houses down from the church, so he decided to take it. Surprising even himself, he moved the car right into the spot. He jumped out of the car and held the door open for his mother.

As Mickey and his mother entered the church, the organist began playing "Onward, Christian Soldiers," and again Mickey's mind drifted to football. He visualized his team being the soldiers and Dalton being the victim of their onslaught. This is getting ridiculous, he thought. Everything, and I mean everything I think or do, is always about football. It is getting to be an obsession. It is getting bad. The season had better get started so I can take my frustrations out on something.

Mickey and his mother walked down the aisle following the deacon. He looked around the church, and there was only one available pew on that side and that is where they were headed. As they approached, he noticed the small pew was occupied by just two women and they looked familiar. Oh my gosh, it was the Bannings. Mickey almost halted in his tracks. The deacon was standing there offering the pew to them, and Mickey was still three aisles away. As Mrs. Daniels started to enter the pew, the Bannings turned their way, and Sally spotted Mickey. She was sitting on the other side of her mother, and she said something to her and her mother stood up.

"Mickey," Mrs. Banning said, "why don't you sit between us, and I can get acquainted with your mother?" Mickey just nodded and started to move around the two women. Then he stopped and introduced his mother to Mrs. Banning. With that, he sat down between the two Banning women and gave Sally a big smile.

"Hi, Sally. We sure meet in a lot of places. Are you a member of this church?"

"Yes, I was baptized here. We seldom miss a service, and Rev. Powell is very good. He has been here since I was a little girl."

"It sure is a pretty little church. The structure is like it is very old and then remodeled without changing the form any."

"That is exactly what they did. They just finished doing it three years ago. My dad said he went to Sunday school here when he was a boy. This is one of the oldest buildings in the town. You are going to find that Fuller is an historic town. Back when they were settling this country, the Indians and the settlers used the two sides of the river to fight each other. Believe it or not, the river used to be deep enough for the bigger boats to get up this far."

Mickey settled back in his seat as the minister began to speak. He couldn't believe it. Here he sat between the two prettiest women in the town. He never would admit that to anyone of course, because he felt his own mother was at the top of the list. Mickey was very proud of his mother and knew that she was beautiful in more ways than one. All the kids in Moorhead had really enjoyed coming to the Daniels' house because his mother was so much fun and always nice to everyone. She had this bad habit, though, Mickey thought. If there was something about someone that she was against, she would sit them down and read the riot act to them, and it didn't matter who it was. However, she only did that when they were in the confines of her own home. I guess, Mickey thought, that isn't a bad habit at all because everyone really respected her for being able to get things across without hurting their feelings.

Like the time Mickey had a few friends over to watch the World Series on TV. The guys had all gathered around the TV and were discussing anything that came to mind. Mrs. Daniels had been bringing popcorn and chips in, and she overheard one of the boys complaining about the English teacher he had and how rotten she was. He could still hear him, and he was saying how unfair she was. His mother just stood there and stared at him. Then she said, "How unfair are you with her? Have you gone out of your way to be nice to her? The teachers aren't always wrong all the time, either. If you don't have the courage to talk things over with her, then it is weak of you to talk behind her back and say the things you are saying. Now be the nice boy that I know you are and go to her and try to explain how you feel, and I'll bet everything will work itself out. You are too nice of a young man to talk behind someone's back."

Mickey could still see the look on the boy's face. The funny thing was, the boy wasn't insulted by his mother's remarks, but actually thanked her for her little talk. He went to the English teacher that Monday and had the little talk his mother suggested, and he said he never really knew that his teacher could be that nice. His grades went from Ds to Bs, and he told Mickey it wasn't from brownnosing but she told him how to study. She also told him to quit staring out the window.

Just then the congregation rose to sing a hymn, and he and Sally were sharing a hymnal. She held one side and he the other.

He looked down at her, and she looked up and smiled at him. Mickey almost melted. He quickly looked down at the hymnal and began singing. The smell of Sally's perfume rose into his nostrils, and he looked down at her again. She was singing for all she was worth, and Mickey made another mental note how beautiful she was. That lucky dog, Billy Brown! Mickey wasn't going to cause any problems, but if he ever got the opportunity for Sally to be his girl, he was certainly going to try. Not because she was so pretty but because she was so nice.

The minister began his sermon by welcoming all the new people in the congregation to the church and offered his services to any of those that wanted to choose this particular church as their permanent church. He seemed to be a nice man of about fifty. His hair was salt-and-pepper in color and his eyes twinkled. Mickey pictured him as an ex-football player. There I go again, he thought. Now I have the parson playing football. The sermon of the day was "Search and Ye Will Find." Mickey knew that was true because his parents told that to him all the time. Nothing comes to those that sit on their hands and do nothing.

While Mickey sat there, Mrs. Banning slipped her hand into his and whispered to him, "How do you like our little church and minister?"

"It is really swell, Mrs. Banning. Everything is so homey. I like the minister. He is nice." Mrs. Banning gave his hand a squeeze and then patted him on the thigh. Then she turned to his mother, said something, and then sat back to listen to the sermon. Mickey looked behind Mrs. Banning at his mother, and she caught his eye and gave him a wink. Mrs. Daniels looked very happy, and he hoped she would be happy in Fuller. He knew it was harder for the older people to make new friends in a town because the kids had the school, yet his mother sat there with a big smile and looked ever so happy. I guess being in church can do that to you, he thought.

The service was over and everyone was on their feet and leaving. Mickey noticed all the people moving about. Then he spotted Chad on the other side; at the same time Chad spotted him. Chad's mouth was hanging open, and Mickey just grinned. Sally was holding on to Mickey's arm and then looked up at him and grinned. Mickey looked at Chad, and Chad faked a slap on his forehead. Mickey kept grinning and walking.

When they got outside, Chad came over to them and said, "Hi, Sally. Hi, Mickey, Hi there, Mrs. Banning. Good to see you again, Mrs. Daniels."

"Hi, Chad," both mothers said in unison.

"Hi, Chad," Mickey said. "Do you belong to this church, too?"

"Yeah, but this is the first time I've been to church all summer. Thought I had better get some extra help if football starts tomorrow."

"Ha-ha," laughed Mickey. "There is a method to your madness. That is why I am here today, too."

"I usually attend every Sunday during the school year, but I sluff off during the summer," said Chad.

"There is a Sunday school class for senior high students during the year, but they just have Sunday services during the summer," Sally said. "Most of the kids do what Chad does. I do the same thing when I feel lazy. I'll be glad when school starts and then I will be used to getting up early. I love to sleep in, and I guess that is why I love summer so much."

Sally's mother motioned to her, and she started moving away. "See you two soon," she said.

"It was nice sitting with you in church, Mickey. See you later."

"Bye," both boys said together. Chad looked at Mickey in disbelief. "I sure hope Billy Brown doesn't hear about this. He sure is going to be angry."

"Why should he be angry about me going to church?"

"It's not going to church, and you know it. It's the thought of you sitting with his girl and walking out with her on your arm. Man, I about died! I haven't seen her with another boy for over a year."

"Well, I guess I had better find a hideout. The bad Billy Brown is looking for me."

"I'm serious, Mickey. You don't know Billy like I do. He doesn't really care about anybody but himself. He is a great ballplayer, but he has a lot to learn about people."

"Let's worry about that when the time comes, okay?"

"Yeah, sure. See you tomorrow. Hey, I'll pick you up at eight and that way we won't be late."

"That would be great, Chad. Thanks. I'll see you tomorrow."

Chapter 3

Before Mickey knew it, his father was shaking him awake and the big day was here—the first day of fall practices. As Mickey thought back over the long wait, he realized it hadn't been as long as he thought. When you want something very badly and you have to wait for it, it never seems to get there quickly. Well, it was here. Mickey had twenty-five minutes before Chad would be picking him up.

When you are in a new town and new people, there are many unknown factors. He knew the first practice at Moorhead had over hundred boys there, but he also knew that it was much larger than Fuller. There aren't many schools around Fuller except Dalton, but it was a nice-sized school. The thought of numbers kept running through his mind. He was new, and he would be at the bottom of the totem pole. How many boys would he have to work through?

Mickey was all dressed and ready to go. He had eaten four eggs this morning and three glasses of OJ. The adrenalin was really flowing through him. He gathered together all his stuff and had it in his duffel bag. I better go through it again, he thought. He took everything out, checked it all, and replaced it. He got another bar of soap because he knew they would be showering a lot, shampoo, too. When he went into the bathroom to get the soap and shampoo, he decided to jump on the scale. He looked down, mentally subtracting five pounds for the clothes and shoes, 178 pounds. He actually weighed 173. That was going to help. He had two milk shakes last night, and his mother had had a great Sunday dinner. If he doesn't keep gaining weight, it won't be his fault.

Mickey had just finished putting everything into his bag and tying his cleats to the handles when he heard the horn out front. He ran to the door and yelled, "Be right there, Chad." He went into the kitchen and kissed his mother good-bye and said, "Stock up the rubbing alcohol. I'll probably need it real soon."

"Good-bye, Mickey. Good luck and remember what your father told you at supper last night. The fight isn't over until the fight is out of the man."

"I'll remember, Mother, and thanks. See you soon." With that he went running out the door and across the lawn.

"Hi, Chad. All ready to go?"

"I don't know. I am never too anxious for the early drills to start. I love to practice, though. A lot of guys hate it, but I love it."

"Yeah, the only time that I don't really like it is if the coach gets angry and you stay there getting punished and punished by each other until you have what they want. Seems like somebody always gets hurt when the coaches keep everyone there just because they aren't satisfied."

"Boy, Mickey, you sure have a lot of stuff in that bag. What all do you have in there?"

"Oh, a lot of sweat socks, T-shirts, and stuff. They will issue us a locker, won't they?"

"Sure, they give everyone a locker, including the JV. They fixed up the locker room this year, too. Mr. Banning is the new Booster Club president, and they built a sort of rumpus room next to the locker room. It is for the varsity football players and no one else. I haven't been in there yet, but they say it is real neat. We have never had anything like that before."

Just then they rolled into the parking lot. Mickey's dad had taken him out to register for his classes but that was the only time he had been to the school. It was pretty for a school. It was built along the lines of a castle. He noticed there were a lot of cars and also a lot of bicycles. Here, at Fuller, the varsity and reserve teams started together in their conditioning and training. When school starts, they will separate them. That explained the bikes. There were a lot of freshmen and sophomores there, too.

He followed Chad into the gym and was startled to see what he did. He couldn't believe his eyes. He expected to see guys all over the place and what he saw was a lot of guys, but they were sitting all over the gym in groups and hardly talking above a whisper. As they entered, several boys came up to Chad and slapped him on the back and faked throwing punches at each other. There was a big group of kids at one end of the gym that looked real young. That must be the ninth and tenth graders, he thought. He checked his watch and it was eight twenty. Several of the coaches were sitting with some of the guys, and they were laughing and carrying on about the next three weeks. There were boys actually sitting in the middle of the floor and along the walls, just talking. Mickey thought it must be a rule or Coach Barron had a thing about noise. Mickey wanted to ask Chad what the story was but he was too busy gabbing with all his friends. Chad had forgotten that Mickey was even there. In fact, there wasn't anyone in the whole gym that knew he was there. When practices get going, he thought, they'll know I'm here. He wanted to start in that backfield so bad he could taste it.

Coach Barron came in at eight twenty-nine and got them all together in front of the scorer's table in the front row of the bleachers. He began to speak.

"We are beginning the first day of an undefeated season." All the guys started hooting, hollering, and whistling. The gym was full of excitement. Coach Barron raised his hands and everything immediately got quiet. He began to speak again.

"I expect everyone to be 100 percent into this program. Anyone who does not give that much of himself will not be part of the program. This team is not mine; it is yours. I am here to help and guide you. Anyone making my job difficult will be dealt with. Any training violation will be cause for immediate dismissal from the team. If you think it is necessary to break the rules to be a big shot, you may be the big shot you want to be, but it will be as a spectator. That is the last time I will mention that, and I hope the last time anyone else even thinks about it. We are going to have the physicals this morning. I want you to fill out the personal information form and do that here at the table. It is just your name and phone number. Now I want . . ."

Coach Barron seemed to be looking right through the guys, and his eyes got rather glassy. He sure looked angry. When his voice died off, all the boys turned and looked over their shoulders and saw three figures come strolling across the floor. All three were pretty good-sized boys and really well put together. In the middle was a very dark-haired, muscular boy of about six foot one. He had that athletic look, the look of the natural athlete. Mickey knew right away that this was a good football player. The three boys came up to the front of the group as if they were expected to do so. The other boys were no little kids. One was about six foot three and was bigger than Randy Mason. He had to be at least 230 pounds. He had a big scar on his cheek that was fire red. His shoulders looked wide enough to lay a yardstick across. The other boy was about the same size but a little leaner. He was about 175 and had the grace of a gazelle. He looked more like a track man than a football player. The dark-haired boy looked to be about two hundred pounds. Gee, he sure was a solid-looking guy. Mickey knew this had to be the great Billy Brown.

Coach Barron was obviously disturbed. Extremely angry would be a better way to put it. Then the roof fell in.

"Listen, you three," Coach Barron yelled. "If you don't think any more of this team than to be ten minutes late, it won't be necessary for any of you to stay. This is a team, not a country club where you can come and go as you please. Now I personally don't care who you are or how good you are. You will follow the instructions of the team and coaches to the letter or you won't be part of it."

"But, Coach, I . . ." began the dark-haired boy.

"No buts. If you want to be a part of this team, you will be like everyone else when it comes to rules and regulations. No exceptions! You are ten minutes late, and the letter said eight thirty, *and don't be late,*" he shouted. "That will cost you three guys ten extra wind sprints after the practice this afternoon. Now, all the seniors, line up at my office door and take your shirts off. All the rest of you spread out and start to fill out the information form. We can get done faster if we can do all these things smoothly and without any undue noise. Seniors, after your physical, report to the equipment room for your gear and locker assignment. Chad, when you get there, tell Sparky that I don't want all the seniors in one area, juniors in another, and so on. Spread them out."

"Okay, Coach," Chad said. "Let's go, seniors. Twelve weeks before Dalton."

All the seniors jumped up and headed for the door. They were all shouting and screaming about destroying the "Red Raiders," beating their cross-river rivals. That is what it is all about, thought Mickey. Leave it to Chad to get them fired up. He really is a leader. Randy waived to Mickey on his way out and that made him feel better now that he was in a room full of boys he did not know, except Coach Barron, of course. He had seen some of the guys around town but didn't know any of their names.

Coach Barron began to speak again, "Fellows, I want you to know that there is no individual on this team that cannot be done without. I am proud of all the boys and especially seniors because they have come all the way through the program, but no one is better than anyone else. You will all have an equal chance to make the varsity. No one will be cut because of ability or lack of equipment. Only discipline or the doctor will cause you to be taken out of the program. I guess I should say academics, too. If there are any questions about anything, ask any of the other coaches or me, and any of you that are new to the school, just feel your way, and I'm sure the rest of the boys will fill you in. Coach Howard will start you filling out the personal information form, and then, when the seniors are done with physicals, it will be the juniors turn and on to the equipment room. Good luck."

Mickey sat there and felt a real warm sensation going through his body. The last twenty minutes had been a real experience for him. In Moorhead, the stars of the team were treated with awe. They seemed unable to make a mistake. The coaches took a special interest in the so-called superstar. He remembered, however, Coach Dawson saying that anyone was expendable. I guess that meant the same thing Coach Barron had said, but it didn't really work that way. Coach Barron was tough, and Mickey liked that. It was the only way to make a strong team.

Time passed quickly. The chore of the physical was over, and Mickey was now in line for his gear. The equipment was strung out all over the big room, and he went right to the helmets. He wanted to make sure he had one that fitted snugly because a loose helmet could really cause problems. He got all his equipment and headed for the locker room. There, Sparky met him and told him to find a locker. Sparky was actually a teacher at the school but was the hired equipment manager and trainer. He had been there for over twenty years, knew everything about the school and everyone in general. He was a little man with silver gray hair and horn-rimmed glasses.

As Mickey passed him, he took off his glasses and studied Mickey as if he were a rare artwork. He followed him into the locker room.

"Say, are you Daniels?"

"Yes, sir, Mr. Gilmore. How did you know my name?"

"Son, I know everything. And the name is Sparky down here. I haven't been called Mr. Gilmore out of the classroom in twenty years. Chad Anderson told me to look for the new kid that looked like the best thing to happen to this school in a long time and save a locker for him."

"Chad said that? He is exaggerating. He is a nice guy, but he's exaggerating."

"He's all of that and more. That is one young man that has his priorities straight and will go a long way. He said he wanted to have a locker next to you so he could keep an eye on you. I don't know what that means, but there must be something to it or he wouldn't have asked."

"Ha-ha! He thinks that some strange thing may happen in this football haven. I'll have to thank him anyway because there aren't any of the other boys I know except for Randy Mason."

"Well, Mickey, Randy is on the other side of you, so you will have both of the boys you know right next to you to start with. All the boys are pretty nice, and you will get to know them in no time at all."

Mickey opened his locker and took the lock that Sparky offered him. Every boy got a lock and as Sparky said, "It just keeps the honest boys honest." Mickey put the powder and deodorant and other small things on the shelf. He had to remember to bring a couple of pieces of wood to make some additional shelves. Sparky came by and took him into the drying room. That is where the equipment is stored and hung to dry, keeping the smell out of the locker room. Mickey was hanging his gear on the hanger, and he noticed all the hangers had the name of each one of the players written across the top in large letters. They were all written the same, so Mickey assumed that Sparky had done the printing.

"Hey, Sparky, are we supposed to have our name on the hanger?"

"Yes. I have been doing it for twenty-two years now. Here is yours. I just finished making it out."

Sparky put the tape on the hanger, and Mickey looked around. The big drying room was in two parts. He had asked Sparky why the two parts, and he said one for varsity and one for JV.

Just then Chad came into the locker room and called Mickey. "Come on, Mick. Several of the guys are going to the malt shop before they go home for lunch. You all done here?"

"I have to hang my cleats up and then I'll be ready to go." Mickey headed for the drying room to hang up his shoes. Sparky had hung his rack up and there it was, M. DANIELS right across the top. What shook him up a little bit was the rack right behind his. It read B. BROWN. Mickey quickly hung up his shoes and went back into the locker room to meet Chad.

"Let's go, Mick. I can taste that chocolate malt already."

Mickey wasn't too wild about having a milk shake because he always had one every night before he went to bed, but then he figured the more he had, the heavier he would get. After seeing the great Billy Brown, he was going to need all the weight he could get. He only hoped he could keep his speed and mobility with the extra weight.

Mickey and Chad piled into the car and two other boys joined them.

Chad said, "I want you to meet two crazy guys. The ugly one is Steve Clark and the other one is Ron Baker. Fellows, this is Mickey Daniels. He just moved into town last month."

"Hi, Steve, Ron. Glad to meet you."

"Hi, Mickey," Steve said.

"Hi, Mick. Chad has told us about you already," said Ron. "Glad to have you on the team, and welcome to Fuller."

"Thanks, guys. Say, Chad, I thought you and Randy were such good buddies? Where is he?"

"Oh, he drove this morning, too. We'll meet him at the shop. You should have seen him getting his equipment. Sparky gave him all his gear, and his pants were a size 36. Randy about died. He started carrying on and faking that his feelings were hurt until Sparky thought he meant it. As a result, he did get size 34, but that was bigger than he had last year."

"I think I can picture him going into his routine," said Mickey. "That guy is really a card."

"You haven't seen him at his best, though," said Steve. "He will crack you up at practice. He is the only thing that keeps me going at these preseason practices."

Mickey listened to the guys talk on the way to the malt shop. No one had yet asked him what town he had come from. That made him feel good because they were accepting him as he is and not where he came from. From the gist of the conversation, Ron was expected to start at guard. He played on the varsity last year and had played a lot. They were discussing the entrance of Billy Brown. Mickey got a kick out of the way they were trying to stammer and stutter the way Billy did when Coach Barron kept interrupting him. Steve really liked the way the coach handled it.

"You know," Steve was saying, "I think he got just what he deserved. None of the young players will be late now. That's for sure. If you see the big shot get reamed, that usually sinks in. He still got all the attention. Man, playing in the same backfield with him is a real experience. Boy, Chad, if he talks in the huddle this year, I am going to say something. He isn't the quarterback, and he can keep his mouth shut. It always makes me angry when he asks you to call his plays. You handle him real well, Chad, but I am going to say something to Coach if he keeps it up."

Mickey felt like an outsider because he didn't know what they were basing their statements on. He always thought teams were one big happy family. He sure hoped this one would be. The car came to a screeching halt in front of the shop, and Randy was there waiting for them. He came to the curb and opened the car door.

"Party of four for the Anderson table," Randy said. "Four shakes and easy on the malt. They look a little young."

They all entered the shop, laughing and chattering about how comical Randy was. Mickey had been there several times before to get shakes but didn't realize that this was the high school hangout. There had been hardly anyone in here when he came in—must be the place during the school year and not so much during the summer.

The afternoon rolled around faster than Mickey realized. Chad's horn was sounding and had awakened Mickey from a sound sleep. He quickly rose and went to the door and yelled, "Be there in a sec." Mickey turned to yell to his mother that he was leaving, and she was right behind him with a glass of orange juice. Mickey smiled, took the glass, and quickly downed the juice.

"Thanks, Mom. Be right home after practice."

"Good luck, Son. Be careful. Take the ball and playbook back to Coach Barron."

Mickey had put them next to the door so he wouldn't forget them and, if his mother hadn't mentioned them, he would have run out the door without them. He picked them up and headed out the door. In the car already were Randy, Steve, Ron, and Chad.

"Hustle, Mickey," yelled Randy. "We have to get Tim yet, and we don't want to be late."

Mickey checked his watch. And saw they had twenty-five minutes.

"Hey, we have enough time," said Mickey. "We have twenty-five minutes."

"No, we don't," said Chad. "I like to have a fifteen minute spread in there so there is no chance that we will ever be late. Coach likes everyone to be on time, and he is never going to get after me the way he does with some of the other hotdogs."

Everyone was in their shoes and shorts. And the new T-shirt each boy was issued that had FULLER FOOTBALL across the front. Each boy had a pair of gold shorts with his name on the left front. Along with the black shirt and the gold lettering, gold pants, and the gold helmet with the double black stripes, the boys started filtering out to the practice field.

Coach Barron's voice came out loud and strong, and the boys began to gather around him. The team was set up in a big square formation, and each boy had a specific partner that was supposed to be close to their size. What followed was one and a half hours of running and drilling that seemed to take six hours. There was no let up. Several of the boys had run to the side of the field and lost their lunches. The team was then divided into three groups and then additional running was done. The centers, guards, and tackles were in one group; the ends and wide receivers were in another; and the backs made up the third group. There are three coaches for the varsity, and each group had a coach. Coach Barron was with the backs, and he was really running them through their paces.

The backs started to learn their plays with about twenty minutes left in the practice and were separated into backfield groups. The wide receivers were working out with the backs because Coach Barron wasn't sure whether he was going to go with a full backfield or if he was going to use one of the backs as a receiver. He had said at the start of the drills that he may just use a split end and not worry about the wide man. Mickey was teamed up with Mike Phillips, a junior quarterback; Larry Williams, a sophomore at left halfback; and Art Raymond, a sophomore fullback. They had Mickey at right halfback. Mickey knew he would be down the line because no one really knew what he could do. While they were standing together waiting their turn to run the play, Chad had mentioned that he couldn't understand why Coach had him in the fourth group.

Mickey wasn't unduly concerned because everything came out in the wash when they put on the pads. The different groups of four were now running the four plays that the coach had given them and were trying to regroup their strength because the coach had said they had another five minutes of running after drills.

As the team was called together for the five-minute running drill, Randy Mason came up behind Mickey and said, "If they run me anymore, my legs will look like Tom Thumbs's."

Mickey broke out laughing. Coach Barron turned to him and said, "What is so darn funny? You can run ten extra wind sprints with the big shots right after we are through here."

Mickey was dumbfounded to say the least.

"Yes, sir," said Mickey. "I'm sorry."

"This is no place for comedy when we are trying to develop the best team in the state."

"No, sir. It won't happen again."

The team went through their five minutes of running drills, and everyone was whipped. As the coaches were releasing each group to the school so they could shower, Coach Barron said, "Brown, Martin, Clover, and Daniels, stick for the extra wind sprints. Line up on the fifty."

Many of the guys stayed out to watch the boys do their extra runs. They couldn't believe Coach Barron had stuck to his punishment. As long as they could recall, they had never seen Billy Brown have to do any extra running, or for that matter, nothing extra, whether it be good or bad.

Mickey lined up with the other three at the fifty-yard line. Coach Barron's voice rang out all over the field, "Set." At that point all four got into a three-point stance, one hand on the ground and the back level. The whistle sounded.

The four boys broke at the sound and sprinted the twenty-five yards that were designated before they started. Mickey thrived on running and his only regret was that he was tired. He knew, however, the other boys were tired, too, and that seemed to be a stimulant to him. He wanted to beat the great Billy Brown, and he strained to go even faster. As they crossed the twenty-five-yard stripe, Mickey was a full two yards ahead of all three boys. Everyone was astounded. They all knew Billy was the fastest boy on the team. He was even the league sprint champion in track.

Coach Barron again yelled, "Set." The four boys went down. In his mind, Mickey said just nine more and set his body for the next sprint. The whistle sounded and the four boys broke into a sprint. Feet flying and bodies straining, they raced toward the fifty-yard line. Mickey knew he had to run faster this time because he had beaten the great Billy Brown. He knew Billy would try even harder to beat the upstart newcomer. As they flew past the fifty, Mickey was a stride ahead of all three, again, and the whispers and shouts from the sidelines were very noticeable. Coach Barron went up to Billy and said, "Mr. Brown, either you start running these sprints or you will run an additional ten."

"But, Coach, I was running. I'll admit the first time I wasn't exactly full go, but I broke my rear end on the last one."

"Well then, can you explain why you can't win one of these sprints?"

"I will, Coach. I will."

Coach Barron then turned and moved back. When Mickey and the other three had lined up on the fifty, Coach Barron again shouted, "Set." All four went down. Billy was really digging in. The whistle sounded and again all four shot off at the initial sound. This time there was more distance between the boys, but Mickey and Billy were still out front and about shoulder to shoulder. As they neared the twenty-five, Mickey seemed to draw deep from within himself and his brain shouted faster, faster. His body responded, and he again won by a yard, quickly coming to a stop. He returned to the twenty-five. He readied himself for the next test. Seven more to go. Could he keep his foe behind him, or was he really lucky to be out front?

He heard the "set" and was ready. The whistle sounded, and he broke even faster than before. He streaked across the fifty about three yards ahead of Billy, and he stopped quickly, again. He was breathing heavily, and his legs were aching. He knew the same was felt by the other boys, but he wasn't going to ease off.

"I think my shoes are a little tight," Billy said. "They bother me."

A voice from the sideline said, "Must have lost the wings on them that you used to have."

Billy turned quickly to see who had spoken, but it was impossible to tell because there were so many there and huddled together.

Mickey again heard the "set" and he was ready. He knew that Billy was, too, and angrier than ever now that he was being goaded from the sidelines. The whistle sounded with Billy getting a little jump on the other three. He had a stride and a half head start, and Mickey was straining to make up the difference. When they crossed the twenty-five, Mickey had won by an eyelash, but it was clearly evident who had won. Then another voice from the sideline said, "Gee, he can't even win with a head start." That infuriated Billy, and Mickey knew the angrier Billy got, the harder he would run. Mickey wasn't even conscious of Martin and Clover doing any running. They were there on the "set" but that was the last he saw of them.

Mickey quickly lined up on the twenty-five and knew there were five more to go. He was off with the whistle and pushing himself to the point of passing out. His body was soaked with perspiration, and the waistband of his shorts was a pool of water. When Mickey crossed the fifty ahead of the rest, the only thing in his mind was there were only four sprints to go. He didn't even remember those four because he was so physically tired.

Coach Barron gathered the four boys together and said, "If you boys make no further mistakes, you won't be running anymore extra wind sprints. I'll have to admit one thing, though, that is the hardest ten wind sprints I have ever seen run. Now jog in and get a shower."

Mickey looked into Billy's face and smiled. He felt good. He knew he made a major breakthrough here on the practice field. He admitted to himself that that was the hardest ten wind sprints he had ever run, too. It was the first time he had ever been punished at a practice, too. He couldn't figure it out. From what Chad had said, and what the other guys had been saying, he figured there had been a little humor on the field. He could still hear one of the boys saying that Mason had kept him in stitches at a practice or he wouldn't be able to take it.

On the way in, he was joined by Chad and a bunch of the other boys. They were slapping him on the back and making remarks about his speed and how he had humiliated Billy Brown. They had never seen anyone beat Billy in a race. Chad took Mickey aside and said, "Mick, I don't know what to say. I thought you did a great job, but I can't figure out Coach Barron. I have never seen him this way. He was different than I have ever seen him."

"You know, Chad, I have never been this tired before. I have always worked hard, and I have been through some tough conditioning programs, but I have never had a day like today. I loved it. It was the greatest day of football I have ever had. I hope that I learn as much every day. I hope that I'm not as tired as I am now, though."

"You amaze me, Mickey. You took everything Coach said without questions or anything. Then you smoked Brown in ten straight wind sprints. I couldn't believe it."

"You wouldn't have questioned the coach, either, would you, Chad?"

"No, I guess I wouldn't at that. I'll bet you won't be in the fourth group tomorrow morning during practice. I don't think Coach Barron could believe what you did to Billy, either."

"Ha-ha! That was fun."

"Yeah, but you didn't help matters between you and Billy. I sure hope he doesn't hear about you and Sally."

"There isn't anything about Sally and me. All I did was go to church. There shouldn't be anything wrong with that."

"Oh, well. Let's shower up."

With that, they went into the locker room and started to undress. Sparky came around and issued another new black shirt to everyone and told them they were to have a clean one for every workout. They would have three shirts eventually and to keep them clean. Dirty equipment means extra wind sprints.

Mickey looked at Chad and said, "You know who is always going to have clean equipment, don't you?"

They all laughed at that and started to pile out of the locker room. As they were passing Coach Barron's office, he came out and spotted Chad and asked him to step into his office for a moment. Chad said, "Go out to the car. I'll be there in a minute." Chad went into the coach's office, and Coach Barron motioned for him to sit down. Chad was uneasy because he couldn't figure the coach out today. He just waited. Finally, Coach Barron spoke.

"Chad, I did something today that I am ashamed of but I think it was necessary for the team. I know that Billy Brown is a whale of a football player. I know how he is on and off the field because I keep my eye on him. I have studied all of last year's films a number of times. I know that in our game against Dalton, Billy said you dropped the ball. I knew better the day of the game and the films show that you clearly made a fine handoff. His attitude has to be changed a little or it is going to affect the team. I want him to know it takes more than just him to make this team go. Taking him aside may be the answer, but I hope he finds out for himself without my having to do that.

"I guess I took my irritation out on him right away and got it off my chest. Maybe what happened this afternoon in those wind sprints will take some of the cockiness out of him. I never expected to see what I saw today. Man, that Daniels is fast, and what a quick start he has. I'll bet he can hit the line faster than anyone we have ever had here. I think he may be able to help us this year. He will make a valuable fifth man in that backfield.

"The other thing is that I flew off the handle at Daniels today. I don't know why, but I was just waiting for him to do something wrong so I could make him run with those three guys. After what you said to me Saturday, I had to see right away what speed he had. He sure has it, and I am glad we finally have a boy move into our town with a little bit of ability instead of what usually happens. I wanted to tell you this because I know you have gotten to know me and that isn't my style or philosophy to punish. Well, see you tomorrow at eight thirty."

"Right, Coach. And thanks for explaining that to me. I was wondering what was going on. Oh, one more thing. I thought I may as well tell you this. I don't want to speak out of turn or speak up for anyone, but I thought it may interest you to know that Daniels told me he was going to beat Billy Brown out of his job. Does that tell you anything about the new kid? He is a nice guy and his parents are great. I am not trying to build him up because you make all those decisions based on the player, but I about died when he told me that. See you in the morning, Coach."

Chad got up and walked out of the coach's office and headed for his car. The guys were there waiting for him, and they were going through some of the new plays they had been given that day. The wishbone offense was going to be a lot of fun to work with, he thought. It was great last year and adding the new stuff ought to make them a real fine team. Now if only nothing happens to rock the boat.

After Mickey had gotten home, he went to his room to lie down. He had never been this tired before, he thought. Boy, if everything went the way it did today, things would be great. Mickey had all the confidence in the world in his speed, but he had wondered how he was compared to the great Billy Brown? There was no wondering anymore. He had been put to the test right away. He couldn't figure out why the coach had jumped him that badly. He was usually very conscious of the things that a coach liked so that mistakes were not made, but he must have really irritated Coach Barron today. That would not happen again.

Before he knew it, his dad was shaking him awake for dinner. "Come on, Son, you can't be that tired, time for dinner."

"Dad, you won't believe it. I have never attended a practice where I was worked so hard. Coach Barron is really a condition-type coach. Our team will never wear down in the fourth quarter. And you know, I loved every minute of it."

"Where does he have you playing?"

"Right now, we are grouped and running through the plays. We only ran plays for about a half hour, the rest of the time we just plain ran."

"Well, where are you playing? Halfback or where?"

"I ran with the fourth unit at right halfback. We are using the wishbone, and I really like it. It is similar to the straight T that Moorhead uses. I think the deception is better with the wishbone. What I saw with Chad Anderson with the ball, our own backfield will be lucky to know where the ball is. He is a whiz."

"Well, let's go eat and put some pounds on that frame of yours."

Dinner was a quiet affair that night. Mickey usually did all the talking, but he was too tired. His parents let it go at that. When they had finished, Mickey and his father retired to the living room while she cleaned up the kitchen. When she had finished, she joined "her men" in the living room. They were discussing Mickey's day. He was telling them about the different boys that he had met and gotten to know. He told them he had met Billy Brown and what a big guy he was. He told them that he thought he had exceptional speed and agility for a boy over two hundred pounds. While he was detailing the merits of Billy, the doorbell rang. Mickey went to the door and returned with a big group of boys.

Randy came strolling in first, saying, "Relax and enjoy yourself, Mr. and Mrs. Daniels. You won't bother us at all. Is there anything I can get you?"

Everyone was laughing, especially Mrs. Daniels. She said, "Randy, that chair over there is for you. It is electric."

Again everyone laughed and kidded Randy about being outdone by Mrs. Daniels in the quip department.

"Mom and Dad," said Mickey, "this is Randy Mason, Chad Anderson, Steve Clark, Ron Baker, and I think Rich Clover? Right?" Rich nodded his head and then Mickey continued a little shocked, "And this is Billy Brown."

Mickey had a little trouble getting the words out. He couldn't understand what was going on or why the last two boys were there. He hadn't said one word to them, ever.

Chad answered his questioning thoughts by saying, "Billy and Rich stopped by and suggested that we stop over and pay you a visit. He thought it would be nice if the team welcomed the Daniels family to Fuller."

This further confused Mickey. Why? Why? He could not get through his thick scull what was going on. The more he tried to figure it out, the more confused he became, so he just listened.

Chad continued to say, "Billy and Rich were wondering if they could talk to you, Mickey? They really don't need a go-between, but they said they didn't know you and thought it would be better if I came along. I picked up the rest of the guys and figured we could talk football."

Mr. Daniels got up and shook each boy's hand and said, "Fellows, it is a real nice gesture on your part. You are always welcome in our home, and Mrs. Daniels and I hope that you use the welcome often. Also, I would like to offer you all a chance to get any of your athletic equipment at a discount down at the store. Don't worry about taking advantage of me because I'll make up the difference on the boys from Dalton. Ha-ha."

All the boys laughed, and Mrs. Daniels countered by saying, "Now that the commercial is over, would you boys like something to drink?" No one said anything but just looked at each other. She continued to say, "I don't believe it, Randy has nothing to say."

Again they all laughed, and Mickey suggested shakes for everyone. Mrs. Daniels winced but left the room to get them started.

"Mickey," Billy began, "I would like to get something off my chest, and I talked to Chad, since he is the team leader, and he suggested that I come over and talk to you. There has been talk around town that I don't get along with anyone and that the people think that I think I am the whole team. Then, today, when we had to run those wind sprints, it seemed to me that all the guys were cheering for or against me or you or whatever. I want you to know one thing right now and believe me when I say that there is one major interest for me this year in football. I want to play well enough to get myself a scholarship to college to play football. That is my major interest, but not my only interest. I want our team to go undefeated, make the state ratings, and then the playoffs. I don't think this will be possible if there is dissension on the team. Any split at all between the players or between the players and the coach will kill most of those chances. I also want to beat Dalton pretty bad. I know a lot of people over there, and they have really been riding me. I want to stick it to them this year.

"Mickey, I don't care who plays, but one of them is going to be me. I heard that you wanted to beat me out of my position and that is great. I want everyone to try that hard. However, you had better set your sights on someone else because I am going to play harder than I ever have before and try to be a team man. My father told me after the season last year, and I say after the season, that he thought I wasn't much of a team man.

"I don't think that is my fault, but if it is, I am going to correct it. We have a great bunch of guys and I like to have fun. What happened to you today amazed me. I have never seen Coach Barron like that before. It was the first time he ever punished me on the field. And to make you run wind sprints for laughing, gosh, I about died."

"Well, Billy, I . . ."

"Wait a minute. I want to say something else. Our entire backfield is back from last year, and I know you are going to have a tough time breaking into the lineup because we are all seniors and you are just a junior, but the way you ran today, there has to be a place for you to play. I wish you all the luck you need, and I hope you take what I have said the right way. I respect your speed. You ran me right into the ground. I don't think I have been beaten in a race for two years. If we both play in the same backfield, the other teams will have a tough time stopping us. Chad is the best quarterback in the state and that will make it even harder on the other teams."

"Billy, I'll admit I was building a rather poor impression of you and it is all hearsay. Billy, all I want to do is play football. Like I told Chad, I want to be a starter. I just want to play."

Randy interrupted the conversation by saying, "I am not usually the one to be serious, but Coach Barron seems to be scared to death about this season. He is different on and off the field. I think he knows he has a lot of holes to fill on the team this year, and he knows Dalton has lost only three. The only loss that will hurt them is Shaw. Billy, I think it is great that you are thinking about the team. We can be much better than many people think. I'll agree with you that the two of you, along with Steve, can knock the snot out of a lot of teams. To hear you talk like this makes me want to block even harder for you than I did last year."

"Me too," said Ron. "I hope I get to start at guard next to you, Randy. I know that I am going to work twice as hard because I want to be in the lineup in that first game with Torrence."

"If you do," said Randy, "I hope you can get that good-for-nothing center Tubby Franklin to wash his socks."

That cracked everyone up. They were all in a pretty good mood. Mrs. Daniels came in with seven milk shakes and started passing them around. The boys each grabbed one and thanked her. She was in her glory. The boys were having a great time, and she felt they were accepting her son into their group, which made her feel very good. They were talking about their team and they were including her son. This was important to her because that is all Mickey has been thinking about lately.

After a while, Billy rose and said, "Chad, we better get going. We don't want to be out after hours. Coach Barron would be mighty upset if he knew all of us were breaking one of his rules. He isn't going to get me in one of those wind sprint sessions, again. No siree."

The boys all stood laughing and headed for the door, thanking Mrs. Daniels for the shakes and telling her and Mr. Daniels they were happy to meet them. Chad was saying, "Billy, you have really made my day. I never knew you felt this way, and I'm sure that no one else knew, either, except for the guys you hang out with."

"We'll have to remedy that, Chad," Billy said, "and start hanging around together as a group. Thanks, Mickey, and good luck on your try for our backfield. I feel sorry for Pearson because I know you will play heck getting my spot, and Steve, here, is a real tough man in a battle."

The boys left, and as Steve passed Mickey, he said, "I don't know what to tell you but that is the greatest piece of fieldwork that I have ever seen Billy do. He never once thanked me last year for a block or patted anyone on the back. He must want a good season really bad."

"See you tomorrow, Steve. Thanks for stopping by."

Mrs. Daniels threw her arms around Mickey and told him, "I am so happy. Things seem to be going so well. I hope things keep up like this. I was so worried for you when we left Moorhead. So was your father."

"That's right, Mickey," his dad said. "I didn't know what to expect. You are changing schools at a difficult time. I hope everything keeps going the way they are. Say, did you lift any weights tonight?"

"No, Dad. I lifted last night, and you don't want me lifting two nights in a row. Besides, I'm bushed."

With that, Mickey headed toward his room and his new playbook. The new one had very little difference than the one Coach Barron had left him on Saturday. There was a lot less to it, too. Coach said pages would be added as the season wore on. It was a three-ring notebook and was divided into separate sections. Number one was rules and regulations. Number two was the philosophy of the wishbone T. Number three was the defensive setup. Number four was the offensive setup and a place for new plays. Number five was the philosophies of other coaches. Mickey went right to section six and began studying. He wanted to be as familiar as he could with as much as he could.

Chapter 4

The next day began with the morning practice. There wasn't anyone late but there did seem to be fewer people. The team lined up with their partners in the gigantic square and did their stretching drills. Mickey noticed how sharp everyone looked with their gold shorts, black shirts, and their gold helmets. They were a sharp-looking group. They were doing things together and very smoothly. Each little exercise had its own importance.

The team ran and ran some more. They were then divided into their groups and went through more individual training drills. They were soaked again, but it felt good. The backfield groups for learning plays were the same.

In Mickey's group, Mike Phillips was still running the plays at quarterback. He seemed to know what he was doing, but he never got to the handoff spot quick enough to get the ball to Mickey. Mickey would have to slow up and that threw their timing off. He didn't fumble but he did stumble a little, and Coach Barron picked up on it right away.

"For a guy that can run as fast as you can, you seem to be a little clumsy," said Coach Barron.

"It isn't him, Coach," said Mike. "I just can't seem to get to him fast enough."

"In that case, you can take ten extra wind sprints right after practice."

Mickey couldn't believe it. That sure wasn't called for. Well, he wasn't going to get away with it. What had happened to Coach? It was as if he was on something and it was affecting him. Mickey and his group continued to run plays while trying to get the timing down. He couldn't wait until they got the pads on. Probably just a couple more days and then they would be in pads. If they had to do as much running then, it was going to be murder.

The practice was rapidly coming to a close. The entire team was doing the five-minute drill. They called it the killer run. They were huffing and puffing when the Coach finally blew the whistle that ended the practice.

"Phillips," Coach Barron yelled, "you have ten sprints to do. On the fifty."

As Mike headed for the fifty, Mickey decided he would do them with him. He was part of the reason for him having to run, and there was an outside chance that if he sided with him, they might get out of them.

"What's going on here?" Coach Barron called out.

"I'm going to run with him. It wasn't all his fault."

"Well, line it up then, Daniels. We haven't got all day."

As Mickey was getting into his three-point stance next to Mike, he was joined by Billy Brown. Then Steve Clark came over and lined up.

"Now what's going on?" said Coach.

"When one of these guys run, we run, too," said Billy. They were then joined by the rest of the backfield. Coach Barron was beside himself. He couldn't make all these guys run an extra sprint session because of one boy's mistakes.

"Let's go, Coach," Chad said. "We are a *team!*"

"Set," and the whistle sounded and twenty-two boys headed for the twenty-five-yard line. What a sprint that was! Mickey and Billy were shoulder to shoulder with Chad pressing close behind. They all turned and lined up on the twenty-five.

"Nine," one of the boys yelled. Then the whole group yelled, *"Nine!"*

"Set!" The whistle sounded again, and they tore off toward the fifty. Again, Mickey and Billy were shoulder to shoulder, and again no one was more than three or four yards behind.

"Eight," came the familiar voice again.

"*Eight!*" yelled the entire group again. They were actually enjoying this even though they were wearing themselves out. This went on until they had run their ten sprints, and all twenty-two boys continued to run for the school and showers. When they got there, Mike spoke.

"Listen, Mickey, Billy. Hey, you guys didn't have to do that. I could have run like you guys did yesterday."

"We are a team," said Billy. "We train as a team and we run as a team. This team is going to be the best darn team in the state."

A cheer went up from the group, and the linemen joined in, too. Mickey knew they were going to be a team, now. Nothing could hold them back.

The boys were in the showers and having a good time. Their spirit was high and highly contagious. Each boy was getting into the spirit of the thing. About every other statement was how they were going to crush Dalton.

Coach Barron walked by the showers and said, "Your spirit is great, but we have to get by Torrence first. They have a pretty good team and are one of the biggest teams we face this year."

"We'll get 'em, Coach. Just a little fodder for our big cannon," said Randy Mason. The place went nuts. Three weeks until we face Torrence. Just twelve more until Dalton, Mickey thought. He was in the spirit already, and he didn't know anything about any of the teams.

The first several practices went by with the team running a lot and getting to know the plays. Coach Barron always seemed to tag one of the guys with extra sprints after each practice, and as a result, all the backs would run. They were down to twenty now. That made five backfields and that is the way they had practiced up until now. Mickey was still working with the fourth unit, and he knew he had a long way to go. What did make him happy was that he was sure that he knew all the plays. This would help him in the long run, and he also knew there were many that didn't know them all.

Coach Barron said that they would pad up for the Thursday afternoon practice, and he couldn't wait. He was anxious to see what was going to happen. It was the middle of the Thursday morning practice, and they were running through the plays. The option play was their main play in the wishbone, and they were working on that when Coach Barron came over to their group. Phillips, Williams, and Raymond were still the boys in Mickey's group, and they were working together very well.

Mike Phillips called eighteen option. He fakes to the fullback going into the line, then moves down the line, and then decides to run or pitch the ball to the left halfback. "Run seventeen, instead," Coach Barron said. The fourth unit lined up and ran the play. Mike faked to Raymond, pulled the ball out of his midsection, and pitched to Mickey sweeping outside to the left.

"No! No! No!" said Coach Barron. "It has to get outside much faster than that or there won't be much of an option on that end. He'll get you both. You have to move. Now run it again."

The group lined up and ran the same play. Everything was the same, and again Coach said, "No! No! No!" With that he came to Mickey and said, "You go over there and trade places with Arnold and tell him to come over here." Arnold was the right half in the third group. Mickey knew he could run circles around anyone in that group, so it was a nice chance for him to move up on the depth chart. He still had a long way to go. The practice ended with the backs doing their extra sprints. They all headed for the showers and knew everything was getting started on a full scale in the afternoon.

The afternoon practice rolled around, and there was a quiet in the locker room that usually wasn't there. They were all putting on their equipment and making sure the adjustments were right. Mickey looked around the room, and they all looked so much bigger. They had trouble putting their cleats on now that they had their pads on. Bending was much tougher.

The team was again grouped in the big square, doing their stretching. There was a spirit of togetherness that had built among them that was very noticeable to those watching. There were spectators today as some of the townspeople and parents wanted to see the boys in pads. There were a lot of drills, and halfway through the practice, they gathered at one end of the field. Coach Barron wanted the boys to get some contact work in. There was plenty of talk on the sidelines because this is what they wanted to see. There was nothing like the popping of pads to get the fans all fired up.

"Coach Rowe, get those linemen into their pursuit drills, and Coach Howard, let's see what the backs are made of," Coach Barron said. The backs were divided into two lines and matched up by size. They were going to have a tackling drill, and Mickey knew this separated the men from the boys. He really liked to hit, but he didn't know what to expect from any of the guys. He did remember what Coach Dawson had told him. "If you want to be noticed and play, hit and hit hard. Never give ground."

He and Chad were paired up, and he was to be on the receiving end of one of Chad's tackles. The whistle sounded, and before Mickey knew what had happened, he was being viciously taken to the ground. Mickey quickly got to his feet and saw the look of determination in Chad's eyes. Nothing was said, but he knew he was in for a real beating if he didn't get into the swing of things. The whistle sounded again, and again he was smashed to the ground.

As he and Chad were getting up, Chad said, "Out here, everything is business. You have to hit or you are overlooked. I expect you to hit me just as hard. That is what we are out here for."

Mickey just nodded. He knew what Chad meant, and he was *not* going to be overlooked. Coach Barron told them to trade sides and blew the whistle. Before the sound of the whistle had died out, Mickey was driving his helmet, face mask, and shoulders into Chad's thighs. He kept driving his legs until the two of them were in a pile on the ground. When they hit the ground, they were at the feet of Coach Howard, the back coach. He looked Mickey in the eyes and tried to see what was there. What he did see was a young back that wanted to play ball. They lined up again, and Mickey's head was still ringing from the first hit. He knew he had really hit Chad and wondered if all the two-a-days were going to be like this. If they were, he was going to be one tired boy but a much tougher ballplayer. When the whistle sounded, Mickey fired across the line and put everything he had into his hit on Chad. They went down in a pile, and as they were getting up, Chad said, "Man, those milk shakes must really be doing something for you. I'm coming over to get a Daniels' special."

Mickey grinned and knew they were helping, but it didn't take the pain out of all the contact. After ten minutes of drills and getting used to the contact, the backs broke up into their units, and Mickey headed for the third group. Tony Rogers was the quarterback and was a small but solidly built boy. He was told that Tony was probably one of the best basketball guards in the area, but the fact that he might get hurt kept him from being a real threat on the football field. Still, when there was no contact, he had all the moves and finesse of Bob Gilbert on the second unit.

Mickey was working at right half with Carl Taylor, the fullback and Brad James, the other back. They were going through the plays, and Mickey again knew he was better than any of the guys in this group, but he had to show everyone before they were willing to concede the fact. After about fifteen minutes of running the option and learning the counterplay, Coach Barron called the team together in the center of the field and said, "Men."

A long silence followed, and the players just stood there, digging their cleats into the grass. "Men." Again silence. It was like Coach Barron didn't know what he was going to say, but then he continued, "It has been a long time coming. I never say this before a season, but I feel you deserve the right to know what is going through my mind." He paused again and then took his baseball cap off and started again, "We have here the best football team in the state."

Any other time, they would all begin to cheer and shout, but the tone of his voice held them in silence and awe. "We have had some super practices so far, and I can't help but feel it's because there are so many good players all wanting to be starters. As you know, only eleven people start on each side of the ball and the toughest job for a coach is to decide who those people will be. As we move toward our ballgame with Torrence, who by the way is really loaded this year, I want you to hang in there and keep working hard. Don't get down and don't give up on the team, this game or yourself. Never let anything keep you from wanting to be a starter. We need all of you, and you will all play. I've only seen us hit a little bit, but I worry about injuries because you all want to play so bad. So protect yourself at all times and keep hitting. I'll tell you one thing, Torrence hits like all get out and they want part of you to hang in their gym. So let's get going and start with the idea of going into the game with Dalton undefeated and staying that way."

With that, all the players were whooping and slamming each other on the back. The whistle sounded and Coach Barron called the first unit over to get on the scrimmage vests to run plays against the defense. Coach Rowe called for some defensive players, and the rest of the squad about ran him over trying to get one of the defensive positions. After all the adjustments by Coach Rowe, Mickey was playing outside linebacker and just waiting for a chance to show what he could do.

The spectators along the sidelines sensed that something was about to appear on the field that they don't usually see because the team was so intense and the coach had taken the time to talk to the team at midfield. The way the team reacted to what he had said had all of them buzzing and guessing.

The whistle blew and the black-shirted first unit came up over the ball. Tubby Franklin, the center, was busy adjusting his stance as Chad started calling the signals. As the ball was snapped, a tremendous crashing sound was heard as the two units came together. Chad faked to Steve Clark, pulled the ball back out, and pitched to Billy Brown. Billy had taken about four steps when he was brutally smashed to the ground. Mickey had sensed the play and came across the line and, with everything he had in his body, unloaded the tackle that had the spectators gasping. Neither boy moved. The coaches just stood there, and none of the team members reacted very quickly. Everyone knew they were hurt but were afraid to find out how badly.

What they didn't know is what was being said between the two boys on the ground. "Holy smokes, Mickey, I'm one of the good guys."

"I know, but I want to play ball."

"You will, man, you will."

Billy got to his feet first and was helping Mickey to his feet as he said, "Nice hit, punk. See if you can do that again." With that and a wink at Mick, he started back to the huddle.

Mickey said back, "Come my way again if the coach will ever let you carry the ball again."

When Billy got back to the huddle, Coach Barron said, "What was that all about? I thought everything was going so good?"

"Oh, it is, Coach. We were just practicing what we are going to be saying to the big boys from Torrence." Coach Barron just looked at him and had that doubtful look in his eye. He wasn't so sure there wasn't some hidden meaning behind all that, but he hoped there wasn't.

The offensive unit came out over the ball again, and Chad barked out the signals. As the play unfolded, to the untrained eye, it looked like the same play again. But this time, Chad didn't take the ball out of Clark's midsection. Steve entered the line and, as he started to cut to his right, was smashed down with a terrific tackle. Again, the two players didn't get right up. Mickey had done it again. Clark was a little slow getting up, and he turned to Mickey as he straightened his helmet and said, "Boy, am I glad you are a Black Knight. What do you have in those pads, steel?"

Mickey chuckled and said, "Must be, but I think it came out of your helmet."

Steve turned to the huddle and said over his shoulder, "Nice hit, rookie."

"If I'm a rookie, you're a rummy."

Coach Barron was fit to be tied. He really didn't know what was going on, but he loved the hitting. The rest of the practice was more of the same, and the crowd was talking about the toughness of all the players. Clyde Lawson, Mickey's dad's partner, was there and could not believe what he had seen. The team gathered in the center of the field. Expecting the team to start for the locker room with the usual moaning and groaning that follows a heavy contact scrimmage, he was surprised to see the entire team spread out on the fifty-yard line and run ten wind sprints at full go. The team was screaming each number they had left like the practice was just starting, not finishing. Then they all got together and yelled, "We're number one champs. We're number one champs. We're number one champs." Then, and only then, did they head for the showers, not slowly, but with the exuberance of kids that have been thoroughly enjoying themselves.

Clyde Lawson fell into step with the coaching staff and said, "Jim, what is going on? I have been in this town for over twenty years and I have never seen anything like this. Those guys hit like it was the Dalton game already and had twelve weeks of conditioning, not two."

"Well, Clyde," Coach Barron began. "I think it *is* the Dalton game already. These guys have been screaming about Dalton since the first practice. You wouldn't believe anything I would tell you. You have to see it for yourself. They have dedicated themselves to an undefeated season, and I hope they are right. This team is so easy to coach. It is unbelievable. It's fun, too."

"Well, I hope you're right about the undefeated season," Clyde said. "They look like winners to me, and the hitting is tenacious."

"You're not kidding," Coach Howard said. "On every play I was expecting someone to get hurt. Plus, they all want to be starters and they don't seem to care who they beat out."

"Well," Clyde said, "I better get back to the store and make some money. The way they are hitting maybe I can sell you some more helmets."

"I know what you mean," Coach Rowe said. "Those linemen have marks all over their helmets already, and we have only hit one day."

Clyde Lawson headed for the parking lot. The boys were in the locker room laughing and carrying on about the comments thrown back and forth on the field. Sparky overheard some of the discussion and asked Chad, "What is going on? You guys are supposed to be lying around and complaining about how tough Coach is, not laughing and asking for more."

Chad turned to Sparky and said, "Sparky, we are going all the way this year, and Billy B is going to do it for us."

Sparky just stood and blinked. He couldn't believe his ears. He had never heard any other teammate of Billy's say anything like that except Cliff Martin and Rich Clover, his two buddies. Just then someone came up behind him and slapped him on the butt and said, "Not Billy Brown, but *we* are going to do it." It was Billy's voice, and then Sparky turned and saw Billy standing there, smiling, and he was even more befuddled.

"Sparky," Billy said. "I haven't enjoyed playing football as much as I have the last two weeks, and we haven't had a game yet. Come on out and watch a practice. If I wasn't in the same backfield with Chad, I wouldn't even know where the ball was. Which reminds me, Daniels, how in the heck did you know where the ball was going? Those first two hits today were as hard as any I have ever seen."

Mickey looked at Billy while he was rubbing his neck and said, "All I know is that I knew that you would be carrying the ball the first time, and the second time I knew that if you were hurting as much as me, they would be giving it to someone else and I guessed Clark."

Steve Clark chimed in and said, "How about guessing wrong once. Man, I can still feel your helmet coming out the back of my shirt."

Chad laughed and said, "Sparky, now you know what our opponents are going to be saying at halftime and after the games."

Just then Randy Mason came up and said, "Sparky, me boy. Hustle into Coach's office and break out the champagne. You know, the good stuff, top shelf. We need to imbibe in some liquid refreshment to regain our strength."

Everyone laughed except Sparky. "You know better than that, Mason, and milk shakes don't keep without a refrigerator. You guys better get to the malt shop before all the girls drink the place dry."

"Yeah, we better step on it," Ron Baker said. "I want to get a shake before I go home tonight. I never seem to get enough to eat."

They all headed for the shower, knowing the hot water was going to feel good. They sang the fight song as they showered. They dressed and headed for the malt shop.

When they got there, it was as if Sparky had had a crystal ball. There had to be fifteen girls, and even some of their parents sitting around with only a few chairs left. Billy headed for the far corner where Sally Banning and several of her girlfriends were sitting. They were talking about the scrimmage, and all the girls had one boy in mind. When one of the girls said something about one boy, one of the others would mention another one. As Billy approached, they all turned and looked with obvious envy to Sally as she greeted him.

Just then, Mickey and Chad and the others entered and the place was packed. The girl and the boy behind the counter were moving about busily trying to keep up. Chad said, "By the end of the season, they will be able to afford an addition and they'll need it."

Mickey looked toward the far corner where Billy was talking to Sally, and he had a pang of jealousy run through him. That lucky stiff, he thought. All these girls in here and she was the sharpest one of all. Maybe some day . . .

"Here's your shakes," Randy said. Mickey took his shake without taking his eyes off Sally.

"You better get those thoughts out of your head, Speedo," Chad said. "That is worse than being the last man between the goal line and Jim Brown running the ball."

"Ha-ha," laughed Mickey. "There isn't any harm in dreaming, is there?"

"Some dreams can be nightmares," said Randy. That cracked up all the guys around Mickey, and he had to laugh, too.

"Torrence is going to have the market on nightmares," said Mickey.

The boys left the shop and were either dropped off at their homes or drove themselves. Mickey entered his house humming the Fuller fight song. Mrs. Daniels was impressed with his enthusiasm.

"I thought you would be dragging after the first day of pads. What has you in such good spirits?"

Mickey stopped humming and gave his mother a big hug, spun her around, and said, "It seems like I have lived here for years. The guys are great and the team is really going to be something. If nothing goes wrong, you will see a team that will make Moorhead look like a junior high team. We may be a smaller school here at Fuller, but we are going to be tough." With that, Mickey opened the refrigerator to look for something to snack on.

"Get out of there and wait until your father gets home for supper. He should be here any minute."

The next several days were a repeat of the first day of pads. The team was getting closer together and was getting into better condition. Mickey worked very hard and knew the harder he worked, the sooner he would get to play. He had been playing on the first unit on defense since the first day, but that is not what he wanted. He wanted to be first team offense. He knew that beating out Billy Brown was nearly impossible. He was really impressed how well Billy played. He wasn't that good of a blocker, but when you ran the way he did, I guess you don't have to worry about blocking too much.

Steve was a good fullback, and Mickey wanted nothing to do with that position. He would play there if asked, but Steve was a shoo-in there. Gary Pearson was a good back, and Phil Andrews, who played behind him, was, too. He knew he was as good as both of them. Gary was there because he started last year. Still, Mickey knew that is where he had a chance to start. One way or the other he was going to be the right half on opening day.

School would open in two weeks, and the team only had one week of two-a-days left. Mickey awoke Monday morning and busied himself getting ready for Chad to pick him up for the first of the two practices. The coach had said this would be a very important week. He would be making most of his decisions on what they did. He wanted as many to play as he could, but he would play some of them both ways. Both ways meant offense and defense.

The horn sounded out front, and Mickey grabbed his duffel bag with all the clean gear and headed for the door. His mother was waiting for him with his usual extra glass of orange juice. He gulped it down and said, "Thanks, Mom. See you tonight. Remember, we are watching a film after the first practice and then have a briefing on Torrence with a couple of last year's team members. Coach is having sloppy joes for us at lunch."

"Be careful, Mickey, and try hard. Did you weigh yourself this morning?"

"Yes. One hundred and seventy. I lost three pounds somewhere. I can't figure it out."

"Never mind. Once your body gets used to it, you will start to gain again. See you tonight, honey."

He headed for the car. As he was crossing the sidewalk, Sally Banning was walking by and said, "Hi, Mickey. Going to practice?"

"Yeah, it is the last week of two-a-days. Where you off to this early?"

"We have cheerleading practice this morning in the park, and we only have two weeks to get ready, too."

"It is nice you are a cheerleader this year. How many . . ."

"We better get moving, lover boy," Chad said. "We don't want to be late and do extra wind sprints, do we?"

Mickey said good-bye to Sally and climbed in the car. Nothing was said for several minutes, and Mickey thought about what Chad had said. Lover . . . Man, he should be so lucky. He would give anything for her to be his girl. Well, maybe something will happen and he would get lucky and have her as his girl.

"Coach said he was going to make some changes today," Chad said. "I wonder what they are?"

"He will probably move Don Simpson to that guard position," Randy said. "Did you see the way he pushed Cal Radcliffe all over the place last Friday?"

"If he makes that move, he will have two juniors at guard," Chad said. "Cal won't like that at all."

Chad turned the car into the school parking lot and parked it under the big maple tree. He liked to park there because it blocked the afternoon sun.

"When we graduate," Randy said, "I'm going to have this tree moved to your front yard, Chad. It is already called the Anderson Maple."

The boys laughed about Randy's remarks, but they all knew that no one parked there because it was Chad's spot. Mickey knew even more why Chad was such a good leader. They all respected him and did almost everything he said or asked. Sparky was right. Chad would go a long way. He told Mickey that he wanted to go to West Point. It was hard to get an appointment to a place like that if you weren't from one of the larger schools. He knew if anyone could do it, Chad could. He thought how ironic it was to feel like he had known him for years when it was just three or four weeks.

The team was just about ready to head out when Coach Barron asked them to leave their cleats off and meet in the gym. They all knew something was in the air. The excitement began to build. What could it be? It had to be more than the usual pep talk or the change of a player or two. Sparky was going around hurrying the team into the gym. They gathered on the floor in front of the bleachers. Coach and his two assistants came in, and Coach Barron got up on the first row and began to speak.

"I told you that we are going to have a good team this year, and our goal was to win the CAL (Central Athletic League) and finish undefeated, ranked, and in the playoffs. I still feel that way and stronger than ever. We have put plays in that we couldn't run last year because we didn't have the personnel. We are better conditioned than we were at the end of the year. You all know that I don't beat around the bush when it comes to the team. We play the best people we can and have no favorites. Tomorrow, the newspaper wants to come in and get some pictures. If you aren't one of those selected, don't feel left out or that you are not important to the team. Everyone *is* important. We need all of you. We have one week before school starts, which means just five days left of two-a-day sessions. I am going to change things around this year and go only once on Friday and that will be an intra-squad game so the three of us coaches can see what we have. We have really gone over the Torrence films, and there are some things we want you to see. We think you can take them, but we have to get some things squared away quickly. The punting chores have been with Billy and Chad, but I think we will use Daniels there. That will take some of the load off the two starters."

Mickey couldn't believe his ears. He wanted to punt and place kick, but the way it sounded, they had no intention of letting him start. Letting him kick was just a carrot. That just meant he had to work all the harder. He knew he could do it, but they had to give him a chance to run with the first offensive line. So far when he ran, it wasn't with the best blockers.

Chad looked over at Mickey, and he had his head down. Oh, oh, he thought. Looks like Mickey is going down for the count. He had talked the changes over with Coach Barron and thought the kicking changes would fire Mickey up, but he knew what Mickey wanted. He wanted in that backfield. Just then Mickey looked up and right into the eyes of Chad. Chad noticed the fire there and wondered what was going through his mind. He had the look of a prizefighter just before the first bell. He told himself he would have to talk to him and find out what he was thinking.

Coach Barron continued to talk, "We are also making some changes in our offensive lineup."

That got Mickey sitting up straight immediately. "I'll have Coach Howard go over those with you when I'm done here, and they will be posted on the team board in the varsity locker room. You have voted Chad Anderson, Billy Brown, and Randy Mason as your tri-captains this year, and I think they are excellent choices."

A great roar went up from the team and the three captains were getting high fives and backslaps by all those near them. Coach Barron raised his hand and continued, "I want to see the captains in my office now while Coach Howard is going over the changes. Coach Howard."

Coach Barron stepped down and, with the captains, headed for his office. There was busy talk again while Coach Howard came to the front and mounted the first row of bleachers. It got deathly quiet in the gym as he looked around at the expectant faces. They all knew something was up or that some big change was going to be made. Coach Howard didn't say anything right away, but began leafing through papers on his clipboard as if to waste time. Still there was no noise. Then he cleared his voice and began to speak, "Gentlemen, I am not one to say a lot, but I have to tell you this so there is no doubt about what is going on. We have a great team here. We are going to have to play together and with everything we have. We are going to have to use all our resources and abilities to be undefeated. Most of you know that the only game we lost last year was to Dalton, and we probably shouldn't have lost that one. This year, we have two new teams on the schedule that are as tough as Dalton, and one of them is Torrence, our first game. Therefore, we don't have as much time to determine our best lineup. We will probably make some mistakes right off, and if we do, we will correct them right away. Don't get down, fight to be a starter. That is what will make this team better. If you are satisfied with being a second teamer, you won't push the guy ahead of you and you won't get to the top yourself. Well, here is the list of teams as we have it right now. Most of you know what they are because you have worked hard enough to be there, but we are making a few changes. At left end, Cliff Martin. At left tackle, Rich Clover. At left guard, Don Simpson." There it was, the first change. Mickey knew that he wouldn't be up there because he never got to run with the first team, anyway. He listened as Coach Howard continued. "At center, Tubby Franklin. At right guard, Ron Baker. At right tackle, Randy Mason. At right end, Howie Grant. At quarterback, Chad Anderson. At left halfback, Billy Brown. At fullback, Steve Clark, and at right halfback, Gary Pearson."

Only one change, and Mickey's mind wondered off as Coach Howard continued to read the lineups. Without knowing it there were four changes on the second teams, and when he started on the second team backfield names, Mickey's mind began to pick up on the present.

"At quarterback, Bob Gilbert. At left half, John Howley. At fullback, Harry Buffington and at right half, Mickey Daniels." Mickey was surprised. He had moved ahead of Phil Andrews on the second team, and he hadn't run with them at all. Maybe they were noticing more than he thought. He didn't want to kick if that meant he had to play on the second unit. He didn't want to play defense for the same reason.

Mickey looked around the gym as Coach Howard continued to read the lineups. He noticed that several of the guys were looking his way and nodding their heads. He wasn't sure if that was approval, but he would find out soon enough.

Coach Howard had finished, and the boys were moving out to put their cleats on. Of the changes, Mickey thought, Don Simpsons's and his had to be the biggest. As Mickey sat down in the grass to put his shoes on, several of the boys were stopping by where he was sitting and said some encouraging things.

"Nice going, Mickey."

"It took them long enough to notice who the best people are."

"Couple more nights and you will be a starter."

Mickey couldn't contain himself. He thanked them all and began to fire himself up for the practice. Coach Barron and the three captains headed out at the same time the team did, and Chad threw a big smile in Mickey's direction. Mickey took that as a compliment and raised his fist in triumph as he jogged toward the practice field. Still, he knew this was not the triumph he wanted. The big one was yet to come, but he knew it would be the most difficult.

Chapter 5

The next several days were more of the same. Changes made here and there and a general attempt to get the team ready for the opener. Mickey had worked hard and so had all the other players. The team was looking great, and they had watched film every day for the last four days. It was Thursday afternoon, and the team had just gone into the room to watch film of the Torrence games again. Coach Barron knew the coach from Tipton, a team in the same league with Torrence, was able to get five films on them. Every time they watched the films, Coach Barron would point out different things he had found.

As they were watching the film that afternoon, Mickey picked up on the fact that the quarterback always turned to the direction that the ball was going. Even if they were going to run inside the end, he would look to that side. As the film continued, Mickey turned to Chad and said, "Chad, watch the quarterback. Every time the team runs to the right, he looks to the right side linebacker first. Same thing when they go to the left. I noticed it yesterday but wanted to see if he did it again today on a different film." Just then another play unfolded on the screen, and sure enough, the quarterback looked left and they ran left.

"See, he did it again."

"Knock it off back there, Daniels," Coach Barron said. "If you have something to offer to the team, then we will stop what we are doing and give you a chance to coach it. That will be ten extra wind sprints after practice."

Everyone chuckled at that because the coach always tabbed someone with extra sprints so they would all do them after practice, anyway.

"Nice going, Daniels," Randy Mason said. "You get ten extra sprints, and you aren't even on the field yet. This is your lucky day."

They all laughed at that, and then Coach Barron said, "This is your lucky day, too, Mason. You have ten extra, too."

They really laughed at that. When it finally quieted down, Chad raised his hand and Coach Barron asked, "What can I do for you, Mr. Anderson?"

"Coach, I think you ought to know what Mickey was talking to me about. I think you might be interested."

"Okay, Chad, or should I have Daniels stand and speak his piece?"

"Coach, I'm not trying to be funny. This is very serious, and you should know what he picked up on watching the film. If I was the coach, I sure wouldn't pass this up."

"Okay, Chad. What did Daniels see on the film that is so interesting and causing so much concern?"

Chad began to explain to Coach Barron what Mickey had picked up. When he was finished, there was such a quiet in the room that all you could hear was the film. Billy Brown broke the silence. "Get another film on, Coach, and let's see if they do the same thing on that one."

"Excuse me, Coach," Mickey said, "it was the same thing on the film yesterday on every play so you may as well check a different film."

Coach Barron busied himself with the removal of the film he was showing and putting on the film he had shown on Monday. The lights again went out and the entire team got quiet. The film was moving a little slower as Coach put it into slow motion. The team that Torrence was playing kicked off, and as Torrence came out of the huddle and lined up, Coach Barron turned off the projector. It was dark in the room and no one was talking. He cleared his throat and said, "If Blair, who is number nine, does this, we will really have an edge. He was only a junior last year, and Torrence's coach says he is what makes their team go."

The projector was turned back on, and the film began to slowly show the Torrence team getting into their offensive stances. Number nine came up under the center, and he looked to the left side of the defense. The center snapped the ball to Blair, and he turned to his left as he handed the ball off to the right halfback. The Fuller team watched in awe as Torrence moved down the field, and Blair did exactly what Mickey had pointed out. After the sixth or seventh play, the entire Fuller team would yell which way they were running. For the next ten minutes and five different possessions, the Fuller team was convinced they had an edge that no one else had.

Coach Barron shut off the projector and said, "Daniels, you will make a fine coach some day. What you picked out of these films will certainly help us if their team doesn't notice the same thing. That probably isn't likely because they will be looking at films on us. Okay, Black Knights, let's take the field. We only have three practices left in two-a-day sessions. We have to make hay while the sun shines."

The team headed for the practice field, donning their shoulder pads and shirts on their way out of the building. They were all sitting in the grass, putting their shoes on as Coach Barron came out of the building. He said, "You know, sitting there that calm, it's hard for me to visualize you people as mean and nasty on the football field. Does my heart good to know you aren't like that all the time?"

"You don't hang around any of these guys, Coach," Randy said. "They are all mean and nasty. Ask any of the girls." They all laughed and jumped on Randy and made a gang pile. A muffled voice came from the bottom of the pile, "Don't hurt little 'ole me, I bruise easily."

Coach Barron blew his whistle and said, "Let's get it going or we'll be late. No one is late or I tack on an extra ten and that will make it twenty." They all hurried with their shoes and raced out to the field.

After the practice was over, Coach Barron called the boys who had extra sprints to do to the center of the field. "Daniels, I hate to make you do these, but I said you owed them and I won't change my mind."

"That's okay, Coach. I was looking forward to doing them. They really help."

Coach Barron called Coach Rowe over and said, "Coach Rowe, you handle the whistle on these, will you please?"

"Sure, Coach. Everyone on the fifty."

The entire team lined up on the fifty and spread out in one big line. Coach Rowe yelled, "Set," and to the amazement of the whole team, Coach Barron got into the line right in the middle of the field next to Billy Brown and Mickey. The whistle sounded, and they all sped for the twenty-five-yard line. Coach Barron was about ten strides behind all the rest, but he was pushing hard. They all turned and faced the fifty, and Coach Rowe again yelled, "Set."

The whistle sounded again, and they all sprinted toward the center of the field, Coach Barron right along with the rest. They crossed the fifty, turned, and were ready for the next one. A familiar voice rang out, "Eight." The whole team screamed, "*Eight!*" The whistle sounded again with the coach right along with the rest.

They had two to go when Coach Howard said, "Is there any doubt about the spirit of this team?"

When practice finally ended, Coach Barron told the team, "Coaches makes mistakes, too. I sure hope that is my last one, though."

Randy livened things up by saying, "That's okay, Coach. If you get in shape, you might beat Tubby out of that center position."

The boys headed for the showers singing the fight song. The spirit was high, and Mickey knew he was at home here in Fuller. What he really wanted was yet to come and the way things were going. It looked like he was going to be on the second offense, first team defense, and the kicking duties. Coach Barron had told him he was one of the best hitters on the team. This, however, didn't help much. He wanted in that backfield with Chad. Boy, he sure could handle that ball, Mickey thought. He hadn't seen many college quarterbacks with the moves he had. He mentally thought of the picture of Joe Montana on the wall. That guy was good. Mickey knew he could be just as good with more training. Chad would make Fuller better, and if Blair was as good as they say, the first game will have two great quarterbacks to see.

All the Fuller defensive players were going to be keying on that poor guy. Poor guy? He was the enemy. If Mickey had his way, he would last one play and then watch the game from the sidelines.

Friday morning practice had been rough. Guys were getting bruised, and Coach Barron called the practice short so no one else would get hurt. They had practiced Friday anyway because the coaches had some things to get in before the scrimmage. Mickey had been blindsided by Randy on a reverse and had the wind knocked out of him. Mickey was glad it was only the wind. He would get over that. Tom Mitchell, the second team center, had hurt his shoulder and probably couldn't scrimmage.

Coach had sent them home to eat and didn't want any of them back until the scrimmage at three thirty. Mickey walked into the house at noon and surprised his mother. "Hi, Mom. Coach called off the film session. I think I'll go out front and sit in the sun and read *Sports Illustrated*."

"Hi, Mickey. I thought you must be hurt. You haven't been home at noon for a week. How are things going?"

"Fine. Will Dad be home for lunch?"

"No, he has to stay and get some things done at the store. They are closing early because he and Clyde want to watch the scrimmage. I think there are going to be a lot of spectators this afternoon. By the way, there is a letter for you on the table."

Mickey headed for the living room to get the letter. A lot of people to watch the scrimmage, he thought. Now if he could just get in that backfield with Chad, all the work would be worth it. Well, he'd keep on working hard and then, just maybe . . . He headed for the front yard wondering who the letter could be from. He sat down in the grass and was opening the letter when Sally Banning came walking by. She came into the yard and sat down next to him. She had on her cheerleading uniform and was truly a vision.

Mickey had a small Band-Aid on his cheek, and she said, "Ouch, does that hurt?" She reached up and ran her fingers over the Band-Aid and looked him in the eyes. Mickey had a tingling sensation from his cheek to his toes.

"Not much," stammered Mickey. "Randy put a good one on me this morning. Where you coming from, cheerleading practice?"

"Yep, we had our big thing today, too, so we can go to the scrimmage. Mrs. Bennett wants us to have all our stuff in order, too. What you got there, a letter from your girlfriend?"

"I don't have a girlfriend. I'm not sure whom it is from."

"Well, I better let you read it. I have to get home for lunch. Bye, now," she said. She patted him on the thigh and got up and started walking out of the yard toward her house.

There was that tingling sensation going through him again. He couldn't help himself. She was so cute in that uniform. Her skirt was swishing back and forth as he watched her leave. She looked back over her shoulder and waved to him. He waved back and again thought how lucky Billy Brown was.

He picked up the letter and began to read.

Dear Mickey,

Our football season is underway, and we have a record turnout of kids. We have a great deal of talent on this team, but we certainly miss you. The kids all said to say hi and good luck this year. They know that you will be a starter and probably the star.

The hardest part of changing schools is making friends right away. I know that won't be a problem with you because you have the ability to make friends easily.

We were reading the paper the other day and noticed that one of the boys on your team is a preseason pick to be all-state.

Billy Brown is a fine athlete. I saw some film on him when he was a sophomore, and he runs well. Keep in there plugging and your usual hitting and you will do fine. Your team isn't one of the teams picked to be in the top twenty, but the word is out that it will be.

I wanted to write and wish you a good season. Send us a few clippings and we will do the same. My wife said she would be happy to keep up the correspondence because she knows the season keeps me pretty busy.

Good luck, Mickey. My best regards to your parents. We miss them, too.

Sincerely,
Coach Dawson

It was nice getting that letter. It made Mickey a little remorseful because he knew that he had an inside track of making the starting backfield on Moorhead's team, and they were class A, a big school. No matter, he thought, I'm going to make it anyway. He got up and went inside and flopped on his bed. He stared at the pictures, and one of them just jumped out at him. It was a 1960s picture of Jim Brown. He was twisting through a hole in the line, and you could see in his eyes that he wasn't going to be stopped. He told the sportswriters that he knew when he was getting the ball he would gain yards. Now, that is confidence.

The next thing he knew was his mother was waking him for lunch. He felt like he had slept for hours, but he checked his watch and saw that it was only thirty-five minutes. He jumped off the bed and went with his mother into the kitchen. He put his arm around her and said, "I love you, Mom."

She leaned her head toward his arm and said, "Thank you, Mickey. Lunch is on the table." There before him was a huge glass of orange juice and his favorite lunch. Two BLTs. Bacon, lettuce, and tomato sandwiches were something he could eat for any meal. His mother could really make them. He ate in silence, thinking about the last practice before school started on Monday. He had gotten his schedule and was happy the PE class was in the afternoon. He hated to go out in the morning in the wet grass, but once he got going, it was okay. You spent fifteen minutes or so trying to keep your gym shoes dry. It never worked, but he always tried. Well, his class was in the afternoon and the dew would be gone.

He wondered about his other classes. He would have to check with Chad to find out about some of the teachers. He hadn't asked before now because all he had been thinking about was football. He better get himself awake or his grades would suffer. His dad told him that he had to do well or no sports. Besides, he wanted to get a scholarship and knew that good grades would certainly help.

Mickey finished his lunch and told his mother he was going back outside. The breeze was great and it helped when it was warm. His mother asked, "Who was the letter from? It looked like Coach Dawson's return address."

"Oh, he just wanted to wish me luck and keep in touch. He said hi. If you want to read it, it is on my bed." With that, he headed for the front yard. It was like the calm before the big battle. The excitement began to build. As an afterthought, he headed back to his bathroom to check his weight. He stepped on the scale. One hundred and eighty-five pounds. He couldn't believe it. He stepped off and back on again. One hundred and eighty-five pounds on the nose.

"Hey, Mom. I did it. I did it."

"What did you do," she asked? "Take it easy."

"I hit my goal of 185 pounds. I've been trying all summer and I did it."

"I believe it, Mickey. All those milk shakes and our grocery bill will bear that out."

"Oh, Mom, cut it out. You know that I had to get heavier or those big guys would break me in half. I think I will shoot for 190."

"For heaven's sake, Mickey. We are all going to have to go out and get a job just to feed you."

Mickey chuckled and headed for the door. There it was, 185 pounds. Good deal. He was still winning most of the wind sprints so it couldn't be affecting him too much. He remembered laughing at Billy when he finally beat him. Billy had said, "Thanks for letting me win one, Speedo. Coach almost put me on a diet. He thought I was getting fat."

Mickey lied down in the grass and looked up at the clouds. They were moving pretty fast with the wind blowing like it was. One particular cloud looked like the picture of Jim Brown. Good grief, he thought, there I go again. Everything is about football. I have to start thinking rationally.

Mickey rolled over on his side and saw a form walking toward him. He thought it was Sally again, but he wasn't sure. She wasn't moving too fast and her head was down. The shape was sure hers, though, no mistaking that. It could only be Sally. As she approached, Mickey sat up. It was her all right. He called out, "Hi, Sally."

Sally looked in his direction and seemed to speed up. She acted as if she hadn't heard him, so he got to his feet and ran after her.

"Hi, Sally."

"Oh, hi, Mickey."

He looked at her and saw that she had been crying. He wasn't so sure, so he said, "What's the matter, Sally?"

"Oh, nothing. Just a little problem."

He wasn't sure what to say. When people are having problems, they either ask for help or they don't want to be bothered.

"Is there anything I can do?"

"No, I just heard some things that have upset me a little bit. I am not sure if they are true or not, but from what I hear, I think they are."

"Want to sit down and talk about it? I'm a good listener. I have about an hour before I have to report for practice."

"Well, just a little bit. I heard the team was really looking good. My dad and I are going out to the scrimmage this afternoon. He is president of the Boosters, and he wants to see the team in action. He loves football."

"The team is really fired up, Sally. The guys are breaking their backs to get better."

"How are you doing? Are you in the starting lineup yet?"

"Oh no, you don't. You aren't going to get me in trouble with you again. I've been down that road before, and I think your mother would kill me this time."

Sally laughed and then looked sadly at Mickey. He wasn't sure what to say so he answered what she had asked. "I'm starting on defense right now, but I still want to be on first "O." I'd give up my spot on defense in a heartbeat to be in that backfield with Chad and Billy."

That seemed to set her off again. She dropped her head and rubbed her eye with the side of her hand. She didn't say anything, so Mickey said, "What is the matter? It can't be that bad. Do you want to tell me about it or do you want me to mind my own business?"

"Well, it's just something I heard, and I'm not sure what to believe."

"If you don't hear it from the horse's mouth, then don't believe any of it, whatever it is."

Sally looked at Mickey. He looked sincere, but then she wasn't so sure if she wanted to say anything or not. Finally, she said, "I got a call when I got home from cheerleading, and one of the girls said she had seen Billy with another girl during the week. I guess she is from Dalton. He used to go with a girl from there, but I don't know if it is the same girl or not."

"Well, don't get all bent out of shape, yet. There may be a logical explanation, and then it could be the girl had seen someone that looked like Billy."

"That's what I told her, but she said she knew what Billy looked like, so does everyone else around here."

Sally was fumbling with her fingers and sniffing, so Mickey offered his hankie. She looked into his face and saw the concern and sympathy.

"Did you have a girl back where you came from?"

"I didn't have a steady, Sally. I did date one girl a few times. I guess I never had time for all that with all the sports I was playing."

Sally wiped her eyes and handed the hankie back to Mickey.

"Keep it until you go. By the way, how is cheerleading going?"

"Fine. We are learning some new cheers the seniors learned at camp this summer. They are really neat, but a little complicated. Did you like our new uniforms? Brenda says the school got them from your dad's store."

"Well, that's good. Now the Daniels family will be able to eat."

They both laughed, and Sally looked at her watch. "What time do you have to go?"

"Chad is picking me up at two forty-five, so we won't be late."

"That gives you thirty minutes. Want to walk me down to my house?"

"I've been told that would be hazardous to my health, Sally. Should I carry a ball bat?"

"Hazardous? What do you mean by hazardous?"

"The guys say you are Billy Brown's girl and he gets angry when other people are with his girl. Chad about died when he saw us together at church."

"Tough! He doesn't own me, and from the sounds of it, he doesn't think I am his girl."

"He's nuts if he thinks he can find a nicer and better-looking girl than you. I guess I'll chance the walk. You don't think your mother will shoot me, do you? Seems like the only time she sees me is when something has happened. When she sees those eyes, I'll be in trouble."

"Oh, cut it out, Mickey. Sally got up and waited for Mickey to get to his feet. They headed down the walk, and Mickey thought how nice it was to be walking with Sally. The sun was shining on her blonde hair as it swung from left to right as she walked. She was truly, truly a vision, he thought. Her figure was as if it was drawn by an artist. Her legs were perfectly proportioned and rather muscular. They were tapered perfectly from her blue shorts. She bounced a little as she walked, and he marveled at her beauty.

"You don't mind if I walk behind you, do you, Sally?"

"You are supposed to be thinking about football," she said with a smile.

"Yeah, I know. That is the first time since July that I have thought about anything else, but you can't blame me. Have you forgiven me about the other night?" She would be surprised to know that when he wasn't thinking about football, he was thinking about her.

"Sure, Mickey. It was as much my fault as it was yours. I can't believe that really happened."

Sally checked her watch again and said, "You still have twenty-five minutes. Want to come in for a few minutes? My mother would be glad to see you again. I think she likes you. Besides, you can have a bottle of soda, and I can show you last year's yearbook."

"Just for a minute or two. I want to be there when Chad comes. He is such a perfectionist. I being late would be a major earthquake."

Sally laughed and nodded her head. "Chad is one of the nicest boys in the school. He and Brenda are the two most popular kids in school, too. They are 1-2 in the class and in the most activities. Last year, when we lost to Dalton, Brenda and Chad spoke to the student body, and they both said they had let their school down, Chad on the field and Brenda on the sidelines. They both said then that nothing was going to stand in their way of this year's championship on the field and the sportsmanship award in the stands. They mean it, too."

As they entered the house, Mrs. Banning came out of her sewing room. She had an apron on and a scarf around her head. She was still beautiful. She said, "Hi, Mickey. How are you? How is football? Are you ready for the scrimmage today? Do you want a soft drink?"

"Fine, yes, yes, and no thank you." They all laughed. Mrs. Banning was looking at Sally but didn't say anything.

"Are you sure you don't want anything, Mickey?" Sally asked.

"No thanks, Sally. Mother always gives me a big glass of orange juice before I leave, and if I have too much, I'll get sick. Coach doesn't like us drinking soda, anyway."

Sally and Mickey went into the sunroom and sat down. Sally excused herself and went into another room. Mickey sat there looking around and wondered what it would be like having a sister. This house looked so feminine, and his house looked so masculine. Maybe that is why Mr. Banning was president of the Boosters.

Sally came into the sunroom carrying her yearbook. She sat down on the sofa next to Mickey and opened it up to the front page. There on the front page, in two separate pictures, were a classroom of chemistry students, and the bottom was Billy Brown breaking through the line. He winced when he saw that because he was jealous. Maybe someday his picture would be there. No chance, he thought. He would have to be a big name in school, and you didn't get to be a big name playing second string.

Sally began sorting through the pages and telling him who everyone was. Mickey recognized some of them, and when he saw pictures of the teachers he was to have, he made a mental note to remember them. Sally was leaning against him and telling him what some of the clubs were, but he was not hearing too much. All he could think of was Sally Banning. He never dreamed he would be sitting with her in her house. He felt so good he was about to explode. He could smell the perfume she had on, and it sent chills down his back. After a little bit, he looked at his watch.

Sally saw him look at his watch and said, "It's almost two forty-five, Mickey."

"Wow, I have to get moving," he said getting up. He said good-bye to Mrs. Banning and headed for the door.

Sally followed him and said, "Good luck today. Thanks for walking me home."

"It was my pleasure," said Mickey. Sally quickly kissed him on the cheek.

"Thanks, again, Mickey."

With that, Mickey sprinted down the sidewalk toward his house. As he was running into his yard, Chad's car was pulling up behind him, and Chad tooted the horn.

"Be right there, Chad." He opened the front door, and his mother handed him the usual orange juice, which he gulped down. Mickey gave his mother a kiss and headed for the car full of boys. Mickey was ready for what was going to be said. He knew they had seen him leaving Sally's house.

"Get in, lover boy," Chad said. "Boy, you do have guts. Not any wonder you hit so hard on the football field. You must be able to endure all kinds of pain."

"Everything has been going so good," Randy said. "I knew something had to go wrong. You can't play football with two broken legs."

"Cut it out, you guys. There is nothing to worry about. She came by from cheerleading practice and asked, yes, asked me to walk her to her home. It looks as if I may live to see another day."

"Not if Billy finds out," Steve Clark said. "I have known him for a long time and he prides himself in his women. He doesn't like anyone talking to his girl."

"He better tell that to his girl then."

The rest of the ride was in silence. Their minds were on football, and each boy was thinking about the jobs they had to do. All Mickey was thinking about was running with the football, and he hoped he had a chance to do just that.

The car turned into the parking lot and, almost instinctively, headed for the Anderson Maple. The boys entered the building, and it was just like game night. They were by their lockers getting into their practice gear, and Sparky was flitting from one player to another giving them their clean shirts. Their game jerseys were being handed out, too, and number 26 was handed to Mickey. It was white, which put him on the opposite team from Chad, Billy, and the rest. They would be in black. *Black!*

What Mickey wouldn't give to be putting a black jersey on right now. Coach Barron entered the locker room.

He said, "Gentlemen! We are going into our last practice before school starts. This is an important practice. We want to see what we really have. We've come a long way since the first day and have found many new faces to fill the holes from last year. It is hard to conceive the strides you have made. We are definitely better than last year, and we haven't played a game yet. This is really our first game. The teams are split so that our first offensive unit is together. After that, it is pretty well evened up. Remember what I told you earlier. Everyone wants to be a starter, so protect yourself at all times, and we are still all one team, so no cheap shots."

Nothing more was said, and the boys were headed for the practice field. They were just about there, and the coaching staff came running out and got them together.

"Listen, boys," Coach Barron said, "there are close to three hundred people over at the game field, so we are going at it over there. Let's look sharp, now."

The team turned like a herd of cattle and headed for the game field. Coach was right, but it looked closer to five hundred. As they entered the gate, Mickey saw his dad and

Clyde Lawson standing by the fence. With him was Sally Banning and a man he figured to be six foot four and close to 230 pounds. It must be Sally's dad, but he wasn't sure because he had never seen him.

Mickey thought about his and Sally's first encounter and was happy he had to deal with her mother and not her father. He would have been frightened out of his mind. He could imagine the sight if he was the one that opened the door that day.

The team warmed up and then broke into white and black groups. Each group had a set of plays and would start on the twenty-five-yard line going toward the fifty. Mickey was on the defensive unit, and the tension was high. Chad was calling the plays. The coaches were behind the offensive huddle. The team broke out of the huddle, and Mickey sensed something in the air, all these people and a new team. A new season was about to start, and Coach Barron was so proud of the start they had made. They were going to start big. Pass! Yeah, good old Chad would like to embarrass the defense right away and get the momentum going.

Mickey got up close to Sam Greene and told him he thought they would start with a pass and to cover the outside. He would take care of the rest. Sam looked at him like he was crazy. Maybe he was, but that is what his subconscious told him. Chad was barking the signals, and Gary Pearson was in motion to his side. That was Mickey's man, and he knew it. He had to take him, but he refused to do so. He yelled to Sam, "He's yours," and watched as the ball was snapped quickly. He sped with blinding speed toward a spot about six yards behind the fullback. Chad was dropping back behind Steve Clark to look for his receivers downfield. Just as he turned around to look, Mickey hit him in the numbers and drove him crashing into the grass.

There was a roar from the sidelines and then from over his head. Coach Barron was screaming at his line and backs for not blocking. Chad didn't move. He just laid there. Mickey slowly got to his feet, and Coach Howard was screaming at Mickey. "What is the matter with you? That is our quarterback. What are you trying to do, kill him?"

Mickey ignored him and went to Chad and started to lift him to his feet. "I'm sorry, Chad. I guessed again and . . ."

"Knock it off, Mickey," Chad said. "That is why you are out here, isn't it, to make tackles?"

"Daniels," Coach Barron said, "get over there and see if you can make anymore stops like that without guessing."

Mickey turned and started back to his position, relieved that Chad was okay. Chad went into the huddle and said, "Man, am I glad that kid is on our team. I never saw him coming."

"Neither did anyone else," said Coach Barron. "Let's just run our offense and see what we can do. That kid will be playing a lot this year. That is for sure."

Chad brought the team out of the huddle and started calling the signals. Tubby snapped the ball to Chad, and it looked to Mickey as if the whole team was headed his way. Pearson dived into the line, and Clark took a fake from Chad and went off tackle.

Here comes the option, Mickey thought. He sprinted wide to take Billy Brown, and Chad had nothing to do but keep the ball. He turned up field and was met head on by Sam Greene. Chad started to spin off, and as he did Mickey came back and hit him from the side and drove him clear into the line with Sam still holding his ankles. Again, Chad lay there. When they had all gotten to their feet, there was another black shirt besides Chad, lying on the ground holding his knee. It was Gary Pearson. Chad got to his feet, but Gary didn't. All the rest of the black-shirted Knights were huddled around Gary, and Sparky was called to get the stretcher. Gary hollered that he didn't need one but he could hardly walk. Coach Howard told two of the boys on the sideline to help him.

"Daniels," Coach Barron yelled. Oh, oh, he thought. What now? "Get a black shirt on and get over here." While Mickey ran to the sideline to get a black shirt, Coach Barron said to the boys in the huddle, "It was only a matter of time before he was over here, anyway. I wish it was under better circumstances, plus I would rather have him running *for* us and not knocking us apart. Chad, don't let him get over anxious, and the rest of you, keep him calm. Let's give him the ball on the first play, get him over the jitters, and see what we all can do together."

Mickey had sprinted to the sideline in search of anything black. Mickey ran around a little bit with nothing in sight. Sparky handed him a black shirt and said, "Is this what you are looking for?"

It was a black shirt with a gold 26 on it.

Mickey grinned and quickly took his white jersey off and tossed it to Sparky. Heading back onto the field with no shirt on at all, Mickey knew this was his big chance. He had to make the most of it. He may not get another chance like this. He felt sorry for Pearson because he knew if they let him play at that halfback spot very long, Pearson would never get it back. He had the shirt over his head but only one arm through a sleeve. Billy Brown grabbed him and helped him get his arm into the other sleeve. "Welcome aboard, Speedo. Let's show all these people what a championship team looks like. Come on, Chad, let's get this train moving." Nothing or no one could have made him feel more welcome in that huddle. The adrenalin was flowing through Mickey now, and he felt like his feet were off the ground. Chad looked Mickey, square in the eyes, and winked. "Lafayette, we are here," Chad said. "Option left on the first go. Ready . . ."

"Break." It was a thunderous sound, the whole team shouting at the same time coming out of the huddle. The team came to the line and Chad checked both sides to see the defense.

"Ready. Set." The team got into their three-point stance. "Go."

Tubby snapped the ball to Chad, faked to Clark going into the line, and then started down the line to the left. Mickey was about four yards farther out, waiting for the pitch. Chad stepped toward the other team and made it look like he was running the ball. Suddenly he planted his right foot and turned and pitched the ball to Mickey, who was turning up field.

As Mickey caught the pitch, he looked up field at what would be waiting for him. There was Lance Peters, the linebacker, right in front of him. He turned toward the middle of the field and quickly changed his direction and headed for the sideline with Peters grasping at thin air and a face full of grass. He glided down the sideline, where he was met by Roger Arnold, who was going to knock him out of bounds. Arnold threw his body at him, and Mickey stopped quickly and headed for the middle of the field, leaving Arnold to fly out of bounds and touching nothing but the ground.

Mickey could see no one in front of him and, in an effort that left everyone speechless, headed for the goal. No one was to catch him or even get close. Mickey crossed the goal line and looked over his shoulder. It was the first time he was conscious that no one was near him. The rest of both teams were reaching Mickey in the end zone and slapping him on the back and his hands.

"Nice block, Martin. Chad, I thought you were running with the ball until it was in my hands."

The black-shirted first team was getting together on the twenty-five-yard line heading the other way. Coach Barron came into the huddle and said, "Now that is the way the option play is supposed to be run. That was something to see."

"That play worked because Chad is a magician. I had nothing to do with it."

"Quiet in the huddle," said Coach Barron. "All right, now run the counter to the right. They ought to be waiting on Daniels, again."

"Twenty-four, counter on the first sound," Chad said. "Ready."

"Break." A thunderous sound to Mickey's ears again. This is what it is all about. It is great playing with these guys. They had all the fire any team needed. They came to the line again.

"Ready." As the sound came out of Chad's mouth, the black shirts fired off. Chad faked to Steve and Mickey going to the left. Billy took a quick step to the left and headed to the right, taking the ball from Chad. Billy flew through the line, breaking one tackle, faked the safety out, and headed for the goal seventy yards away. He looked like he had jets in his shoes.

As Mickey got to his feet, he saw that Billy was only ten yards from the other end zone. He couldn't believe it. Two touchdowns in a row and both for seventy-five yards. The team was sprinting toward Billy, and when they got to the end zone, he got the same treatment Mickey had received.

When they got in the huddle again, Billy said, "Thanks you, guys. That is the first time since I have been playing ball that anyone has ever congratulated me for something I did. But like Mickey said, Chad, you made it work, and that was a great fake, Mickey. I couldn't believe there wasn't anyone there to tackle me. Those were some great blocks, you guys."

"What is this, the mutual admiration society?" said Coach Barron. "We have nine games and a week of practice to go. Now let's cut the gab and play football."

The team went about their business of running the football. As they moved up and down the field, the three coaches huddled behind the offensive team.

"Can you believe this team?" Coach Rowe said. "They are playing like it is the end of the season. Sure hope they keep it up."

"It's as if they have something to prove," Coach Howard said. "They all play together, and there is none of that all-for-me attitude that we had last year. That was a major breakthrough with Brown. Chad has this team totally under control."

Coach Barron listened to the two coaches and grinned. He had been coaching a long time, but he never had a team that did things together like this one. Even Billy was playing like a team man. When he spoke up in the huddle after that first run, he had to look twice to see that it was Billy talking.

The scrimmage lasted an hour and a half, and there were only minor injuries with the exception of Gary Pearson. During the last part of the scrimmage, when Coach Barron put the first offensive unit back in, Gary Pearson limped out behind the huddle and offered encouraging words. This seemed to make them play even harder. The people watching the scrimmage, who hadn't seen the team practice so far, were asking who the new kid was. Most of the people knew that Fuller had started mostly seniors last year and that thirteen of them were on the starting teams. To see them play like this was a real treat to the fans.

The practice came to a close, and Coach Barron gathered them near the sideline. They were near the spectators, and most of them could hear what he said.

"Gentlemen, school starts Monday, and we are going into afternoon practices only." A huge cheer went up, and Coach signaled them to be quiet. "We have a pretty good team here. We have to hit the books hard right away. No sluffing off because we want student athletes and not just athletes."

Mickey thought how alike he and Coach Lawson were. He loved coaches like that. They believed in all the things that he and his parents did. Coach Barron was a little different, but he really liked him. "I think we know who and where we are going to play people to start with," Coach Barron continued, "but that doesn't mean we aren't going to change our minds if we need to. Don't give up on being a starter. That is what is making this team as good as it is. We know we have been pumping you up, but you deserve it. Now you have to prove to your opponents how good we are. Anyone who was injured out there this afternoon is to see me in the locker room. Since you did so well, there are no wind sprints."

A howl went up from the team, and it was like they had won the championship. Chad whistled to get the attention of the team, and they quieted down. "Billy, Randy, and I talked about things that we have been doing together, and we feel we didn't do well enough so we are giving ourselves ten sprints. Let's go, Knights, on the fifty."

There wasn't one complaint. They all headed for the fifty, and Randy shouted, "Coach Barron, you look all tuckered out from that workout so you can skip the sprints. Would you like to do the honors with the whistle?"

They all cheered, and the very familiar "set" rang over the field. The Black Knights of Fuller went into their three-point as one unit. The whistle sounded and the players sprinted toward the twenty-five. They sped by the twenty-five, turned quickly, and lined up on the line. Again a familiar voice yelled, "Nine," and the team responded with *"nine."* "Set," and the whistle. This kept up to the amazement of those watching. They had just witnessed a team hit for ninety minutes, and they were punishing themselves with sprints. These were no ordinary sprints, either. They were running hard and enjoying it.

After the tenth sprint, the team headed for the school. When they got to the gate, many of the spectators were offering congratulations, and many parents were giving players hugs, grins, winks, and all the congratulatory things that go on.

The locker room was a happy place, and the boys were talking about the scrimmage. Chad went to Gary Pearson's locker, where he was sitting with his head down. He had taken a shower and sat on the bench with a towel wrapped around his waist.

Chad spoke first, "How is the leg, Gary?"

"It really hurts, Chad. I hope it isn't going to be serious. I can't even put much weight on it. What does that sound like to you?"

"I'm not sure, it could be anything. How in the heck did you do it?"

"I faked into the line, and as I was going down, it felt like the whole line fell on the back of my leg and it twisted."

Billy came up just then and sat down next to Gary and said, "That's a tough break, Gary. You better get in to see Coach right away. He likes to take care of those things first."

"Yeah, I better." He got up and limped toward Coach Barron's office. Mickey was coming out of the shower when Gary limped by. "How's the leg, Gary? I hope it is nothing serious."

"Me too. You really looked good out there today, Mickey. You sure can fly."

"Well, get that leg healed so you can too."

Gary limped toward the Coach's office, and he thought that Mickey really meant that. Mickey headed for his locker and got dressed. He wanted to play real bad, but he didn't want anyone to get hurt, either.

As the boys were leaving the locker room and entering the gym, there were several people there that had been at the scrimmage. It looked like his dad on the other side, and Mickey headed in his direction.

"Hi, Dad. How did you like the scrimmage?"

"Wow! Your team looks great. You should definitely be a contender this year."

"They really hit, don't they, Dad? After we left Moorhead, I thought coming here would be a step down, but I'm telling you, it's a step up. I think we can beat Moorhead."

"You'll never know, Mickey. I stayed after to give you a lift home. We are having guests for dinner."

Mickey went back to the group and told Chad he was going home with his dad and then headed back to where he was standing. He wondered who the mystery guests were? Probably some of his dad's friends from the store.

As they went outside, the air hit him, and he noticed it was getting a little cooler than usual. He knew that football was in the air because the trees and leaves always made him think of it. He looked up at the sky, and it was clear blue. It would be light for another three hours, and he knew that wouldn't last long, either. It was usually dark by eight during football season. He couldn't wait to go out to the game field under the lights.

Suddenly Mickey stopped. His father walked on a few steps before he realized Mickey had stopped. "What's the matter?" he asked.

"Nothing. I just realized that I am now on the first offensive team. That is until Gary gets better."

"You looked like a first teamer to me, Son. You guys look like you have been playing together for years."

"I'm on the first team. Wow! I have worked so hard for this since that night with Sally Banning and our little disagreement. I wanted to take Billy Brown's place but that doesn't matter. I don't think anyone can take his place, anyway."

"He is a fine ball carrier. Some college will be lucky to get him. By the way, that is who is coming to dinner. I sat with Fred Banning at the scrimmage. Did you know he played for state? He played right half on their team about twenty years ago."

"Sally and her parents are coming to our house for dinner? You have to be kidding?"

"We're going to grill hamburgers outside. She sure is cute, isn't she?"

"You can say that again."

"She sure is cute, isn't she?"

"Oh, cut it out, Dad. And no smart remarks while they are there. That's all I need."

"Well, come on then, and let's get home. Your mother is probably wondering where we are."

Mickey and his dad got in the car and headed home. Mickey was already daydreaming about the football team again. He pictured himself ripping through the line and scoring on a long run, which he actually had done that today. Actually, he had scored several times. Now he had to do that against Torrence.

Mickey and his dad entered the house and were met by Mrs. Daniels. She handed each of them, something to take outside and gave them several instructions. She was always the boss around the house, and Mickey likened her to a coach.

She always had things just right. He hoped that the girl he married was just like her.

Mickey took his tray outside and began to set up the lounges and chairs. When he was done, he stretched out in one of the lounges. That's where he was when he heard the voices inside. The thought of Sally here was as exciting as scoring a touchdown, he thought. Some comparison, comparing Sally Banning to a touchdown. Now that was ridiculous.

The next thing he knew, Sally was standing at the foot of the lounge. Mickey tried to scramble to his feet and was fumbling all over the lounge.

"It is a good thing they don't have these lounges on a football field. You wouldn't be on the fourth team," Sally said as she sat down on the foot of the lounge. She had a huge grin and was looking him up and down. "You don't look any worse for wear, Mickey. You really looked good out there today. I didn't know you were *that* good."

"I don't know what kind of a player I am, Sally, but when you play with all those guys, it's a lot easier to look good."

"That's not true all the time," said a deep voice from behind him. It was Fred Banning. Mickey tried to scramble to his feet again, but Fred motioned him to sit down and extended his hand.

"That is my dad," said Sally. "He has been dying to meet you all day."

"That's true, Mickey, I have. Sally has done nothing but talk about you for the last two weeks. When she said you were starting on defense, I knew it would be fun to have a neighbor on the team. I can get all the inside information before and after the games."

"I'll be glad to fill you in all I can, Mr. Banning. Dad said you played for state. I'll bet that was a thrill in itself. Some day I hope to play on a college team."

"When that time comes, just let me know. I know a few people in the football circles, and I may be able to help you.

"Wow! Thanks. By the way, how did you like the scrimmage? Do you think the team looks as good as last year? I can't compare it because I wasn't here."

"You look as good and better in some respects. You have better team speed, and you are certainly in better condition. That was some run you made today. How many times did you score, anyway?"

"Billy four times, me twice, and Chad once. Wasn't that a great run Chad made when they chased him out of the pocket? I was trying to block for him, and he was running all over the place. The move he made on Rogers was beautiful."

Mickey's mother and Mrs. Banning came outside, carrying trays of hamburgers and buns. Mrs. Banning came up behind Mickey's chair and leaned over and kissed him on the forehead.

"Hi, Mickey. Have you been behaving yourself lately?"

"Yes, ma'am! I have been on my special behavior. Playing football tends to keep me straight."

"That's good. You were great out there today."

"I didn't know you were there, too. I didn't see you."

"I was sitting with the cheerleading mothers. It is a yearly thing for us at the scrimmage so we can get to know each other. We all know each other, anyway."

Mickey's forehead burned where Mrs. Banning had kissed him. He tingled all over. He wondered what it would be like for Sally to do that to him.

"Come and get 'em," Mrs. Daniels yelled.

They all got their food and found a place to sit down. Mickey quickly got back in his lounge as the others were getting their fixings for their hamburgers. He watched as they all moved around the table and marveled at the acceptance the Bannings had made toward his mom and dad. It was as if they had been friends for a long time. Sally got her food and headed back toward Mickey. Her blonde hair was a little wind blown, and it made her even prettier. She again sat down on the foot of the lounge.

"You don't mind, do you?"

"No, not at all."

He was happy she chose to sit close to him. He watched her eat and the way she moved. Now here was one beautiful girl. She is even beautiful while eating.

The evening wore on and the two couples were talking about the neighborhood and various other things grown-ups chat about. Mickey and Sally had since gotten up and gone out front to sit on the steps.

"Well, did you find out what you wanted to about Billy and his phantom girlfriend?"

"Yes, I did, and she is no phantom."

"You're kidding?" Mickey said in amazement.

"No, he stopped by right after you left and was there for about ten minutes. He told me all about it. The night before, that is. I guess he wants to break it off. He said he still would like to date, but he didn't want to go steady."

"You mean he . . . ," Mickey's voice trailed off. He couldn't believe it. This truly was his lucky day. It was a day of him getting all his wishes at the same time.

It was getting late, and the Bannings were getting ready to walk home. The two families said their good-byes, and Sally and her parents headed down the sidewalk. Sally stopped and turned around. "Hey, Mickey, would you like to go to church with me on Sunday?"

"Yeah, sure, I'd love to. Hey, I'll probably see you tomorrow."

Mickey turned and headed into the house. As he passed his mom and dad, they were smiling at him.

"Aw, cut it out. I just asked her to go to church. In fact, she asked me."

Mickey continued into the house and headed for his room. Time to check his weight again. He climbed on the scale and it read 185. Great, he hadn't lost any weight today and that meant it would stay on. He felt so good physically that he took a big breath and then laid down on his bed.

He stared at the picture of Butkus again. Most of the guys didn't even know who that was. He is the greatest Chicago Bear, ever. He really knew how to play. He didn't care what happened to himself; he just loved to hit people. He said it was his mission to take out all the backs on the other team. He wondered if Torrence had anyone like that?

He drifted off to sleep, and his mother came in with a big milk shake and told him he had better get into his pj's and get some sleep. He wasn't sure he had room for the shake but knew he had to drink it. He thought they were a part of the reason he was doing so well. He felt solid and knew the additional weight helped.

Chapter 6

The weekend passed rapidly. Mickey had taken Sally to church. He felt like a king with the prettiest lady in the land on his arm. It went too fast, he thought. It was Monday morning, and he had gotten up early so that he had plenty of time to get ready for school. He was a junior, now. He thought back, and it was like yesterday he was going into the seventh grade and was going to try out for the football team. Now he was a junior, and if Gary Pearson wasn't any better, he was going to be the starter Friday night.

He hurried through breakfast and readied himself for Chad, who had said he would pick him up. He was apprehensive about the first day. He knew a lot of the boys, but that wasn't like going to classes in a new school and all. Everyone would be looking at him and asking him his name. He would have to figure out who the good kids and the not so good ones were. That wouldn't be too hard because the bad ones stand out like thorns on a cactus.

Mickey managed to get through the day because some of the players introduced him all the time. The days passed, and the practices after school were much easier and more geared toward the game with Torrence. The team was thoroughly schooled on the little giveaway that their quarterback, Blair, did. They knew what to expect and were not to yell the direction the play was going so they wouldn't figure out how they knew. He couldn't wait for Friday night. The game is what it is all about. The first game is like an eternity getting here. Then, all the others went by so quickly. They had four or five weeks to prepare for Torrence and then just one for all the others.

It was Thursday night, and the team was entering the locker room for the final practice before the game. They always practiced at night on Thursdays to get used to the lights. It was much different catching a pass at night than during the day, punts, too!

The game uniforms were laid out on the bench before each player's locker—new socks with two black stripes, clean T-shirt with the uniform, and the game shoes under the bench. He knew the same would be true tomorrow night, except the shoes would all be shined and ready to go. No one was talking but were moving about doing the things needed to get ready for practice. The same thing would happen tomorrow night with much more detail. They checked shoestrings, pad laces, chin straps, pads, extra pads, and their helmets.

Gary Pearson came in walking with crutches. The guys gathered around him and wanted to know what the doctor told him. Coach Barron insisted on him having it checked after he spent two days in the whirlpool with the knee not responding.

"The doctor says I have a strained knee. He doesn't think there is any damage to the tendons, but I have to be careful this week because they might tear."

"How long before he says you can play?" Ron Baker asked.

"He didn't say. All he said was don't do any turning motion on my toe. I think I might have to have an MRI."

"Take care of it," Chad said. "We want you healthy and not with a ruined knee."

Gary moved over to Mickey's locker and sat down next to him. Mickey moved his gear so he could sit. Gary extended his hand toward Mickey and said, "I don't know how long it would have been before you got to play in my place, but I want you to know that I wish you all the luck in the world and just do a good job. These are great guys, and you will have more fun than you can imagine. You run like Barry Sanders, and they are going to play heck keeping up with the four of you. I can't play, and I really want to, but since I can't, you have to play for me. Just do me a favor. Get me a TD right off the bat. Make Torrence remember our game more than any others they play, okay?"

"Thanks, Gary. You're an all right guy. You know that you would still be number one if you hadn't been hurt because you are a good player, too. Take care of your leg, and I'll do my best."

"Well, if you don't do your best, they will put Randy Mason there and show you guys how to really run."

They all laughed, and Mickey didn't know whether to laugh or cry. He had a tear in the corner of his eye. He knew that could be him on crutches. That is why Coach always says to make every play like it may be your last and to protect yourself.

Coach Barron came in and started going over the award program. He said that each player would get a little football to paste on the helmet for outstanding achievements they had during the game. He posted a large white piece of cardboard with all the categories you could win a football with on the wall. When he climbed down from the chair, after taping the chart on the wall, all the players looked at it. He had taped it under the sign that said QUITTERS ARE PLAYERS WITHOUT GUTS.

The team was ready, and the Coach yelled, "Let's go, Knights." The team headed for the game field. The band was just finishing up there, and they made a chute for the team to run through. As the tri-captains got close, they started to play the Fuller fight song. Mickey had only heard it from the team, and this sent chills down his back. Wow, he thought, this is only Thursday night. This was as exciting as Michigan-Ohio State.

They went through their pregame and did their Blair recognition assignments. They were certainly ready. The night air was cooler, and they were getting anxious to be done. They were all sky high. Finally, Coach blew the whistle to end practice. They were on the end zone line, and Coach Barron spoke.

"Gentlemen, this is the line Torrence is not to cross. We are going to cross it many times. Make sure nothing gets in your way of thinking football tomorrow night, but tomorrow in school, it is all books. They are going to have a pep rally for us last hour so you can start thinking football then. Most of you will probably play this game ten or twelve times in your mind tonight, but when you do, *win*."

With that the team jumped up and started yelling, "We're number one champs. We're number one champs." They yelled that all the way to the gate and, when they got there, started singing the fight song. They sang it all the way to the school, holding their hand in the air signaling they were number one.

Sparky was there, collecting game jerseys and pants. They had to be washed again as the team got a little carried away hitting. Mickey could hardly wait for the next night.

When Mickey was leaving the gym to go home, Sally was waiting for him along with a lot of other girls. She ran up to him and asked him if he could take her to the malt shop.

"Sure," said Mickey. "I don't have a car, but I think Chad and Brenda are going there anyway, and Chad was going to take me. I'll ask him. Wait here."

Mickey jogged off to where Chad and Brenda were standing and said, "Knock, knock. It's the right halfback calling."

Chad turned and said, "Okay, Mickey, we're coming."

"I'm not trying to hurry you, Chad. All I want to know is if Sally can go with us to the shop?"

"You have to be kidding?"

"No, I'm not. Besides, haven't you heard? Billy has broken off the steady stuff. You don't think I'm crazy, do you? She asked *me*, anyway."

"I'm not so sure you aren't crazy, but sure, Mickey. If you want to risk it, I guess I can. We'd be glad to take her."

"Thanks. We will be over by the Anderson Maple when you are ready to go."

Mickey went back to Sally and told her everything was set, and they headed for Chad's car. When they got there, Mickey helped Sally onto Chad's fender, and they chatted about the team, the cheerleaders, and whatever came into their heads. Mickey was feeling real good about going anywhere with Sally. When they had gone to church last Sunday, he knew that everyone in the place was looking at them. It was like being in Hollywood and going someplace with the star of the biggest hit of the year.

Brenda and Chad got into the car, and they all piled in. Randy Mason had a date with Sue Townsend. She was a cheerleader, too. They had been going together off and on for about four years, but there was nothing permanent about their relationship. They were both seniors now and they seemed to like each other better than before, but they weren't letting on that they were serious. It was crowded in the car, but none of them seemed to mind. They talked about the upcoming game and what the cheerleaders had planned for the pep rally.

Chad pulled the car into a space on the other side of the street, and they all got out. As they were waiting at the curb for several cars to pass, a man came up to them and addressed Chad.

"Hi, Chad, how are things going?"

"Pretty good, Mr. Richmond."

The man was Ron Richmond, a sportswriter for the *Daily News*. Fuller didn't have a newspaper, but Dalton did and served both towns. That is where Ron Richmond was employed. Most of the people in Fuller thought the paper was biased, but the sports fans that really knew anything knew that the newspaper was pretty good to them, too. They covered all the teams in the area.

"Could you give me a minute, Chad?" he asked. "I tried to catch you at school, but Coach Barron said this is where you guys were headed and said it would be okay to talk to you. He also said to not give the opponent anything to hang on their bulletin board."

"Sure," Chad said. "What do you want to know?"

"Well, I've seen several of your practices, and I know the team is really wound up. How do you think your team will do tomorrow night?"

"We'll win."

"Is that all?"

"That's all we want to do, Mr. Richmond. We want to go all the way just like every other team. But one thing you can say and you will get the same answer from anyone else on the team. We want to go all the way, be ranked, win league, and make the playoffs. Plus, we want some of our players to make all-state. You can help us there, Mr. Richmond, can't you?"

"You guys give us something to write about and you will be noticed in the state. After the seasons Fuller and Dalton had last year, it is going to be difficult to overlook you two. How is Billy Brown looking?"

"Super. He is better this year already, and he has a much better attitude. Wait 'till you see him in action. We have a couple of other guys that are playing well, too. You'll hear about them soon enough."

"Yeah, and Chad Anderson is one of them," Randy Mason said. "He is the best quarterback in the state and you know it."

"Well, Todd Blair is no slouch," Richmond said.

"You can say that again," Chad said. "We are looking forward to playing against him. It's a good thing he is on a class A team, gives some of us other quarterbacks a chance."

"I'm covering your game tomorrow night, Chad. Is there anything I should look for?"

"You will be looking at the best class B team in the state and probably the fastest, too. Well, we have to go because we only have a few minutes before curfew, and you know Coach Barron."

The kids waved good-bye to the reporter and headed for the shop. The place was packed, and Mickey wondered what it would be like after they beat Torrence.

The next morning, Mickey awoke ten minutes before his alarm went off. He lay there looking around his room, and he scanned all the pictures on the wall—the older players: O. J. Simpson, Gayle Sayers, Jimmy Brown, and Paul Hornung. Then the newer ones: Barry Sanders, Eric Dickerson, Walter Payton, and many more. They were from all eras and different teams, but they were all running backs. He had saved them for a long time, and he never seemed to get tired of looking at them and dreaming about his picture being among them some day. Then there was Butkus and the big hit. This was football. He hoped Torrence didn't hit like that. He knew they were big but that didn't tell him about them as hitters. Oh, well, he thought, he always tried to hit hard, too.

It was time he got on the move. It was the big day, the opening game. He dressed hurriedly and went to the kitchen for his breakfast. His father was already there eating bacon and eggs, but Mickey wasn't too hungry.

"Your mother and I are going to the game with the Bannings tonight. Are the boys ready for Torrence?"

"I really think so. We have had four weeks to prepare, and if they don't catch on to what we know about their quarterback, we should have an edge."

"The paper picks Torrence by two touchdowns. I guess they have their own way of doing things. They think Blair will be the difference."

"Blair *is* the difference, Dad. He is our key. Besides, Chad is the best quarterback in the state, not Blair."

"Well, Son, hit the books today and then hit like mad tonight. Good luck."

"Yes, good luck, honey," his mother said. "Here, drink up your orange juice."

The horn sounded out front, and Mickey kissed his mother good-bye, slapped his dad on the back, and ran to Chad's car.

The day passed quickly with the pep rally finishing off the day. The team had been introduced and the starting lineups. The thrill of hearing his name in the backfield couldn't be greater than winning an Olympic medal. Now all he had to do is prove to all the people that didn't know him he belonged there.

The team had gone to church together after school and had a meal the Boosters prepared. Following that, they had gone to the locker room to get taped and lay out their gear for the game next to their uniform. The coach told them to get all their equipment on minus their shoulder pads and helmet and meet in front of the chalkboard to go over last-minute assignments.

They had all assembled there, and Coach Barron cleared his throat and began.

"Gentlemen, this is the night we have been working so hard for. There will be at least eight more nights just like this, but Torrence is first. We take them one at a time. They are big and they hit. The papers pick them by thirteen points. There isn't a team we play thirteen points better than us. In fact, there isn't a team we play better than us. We just have to prove it nine times. The game will depend on mistakes. Make them have more than us."

With that, Coach Barron went over several blocking assignments and what they wanted to do on defense.

Pregame was over and the team was gathered on the sideline while the tri-captains were at midfield for the toss of the coin. Mickey was standing off to one side thinking about the game. He noticed how big several of their players were. Randy Mason was one of the biggest on their team, and he looked small compared to the two guys in the center of the field.

Fuller won the toss and elected to receive. Can't score without the ball, he thought. Randy, Billy, and Chad came toward the sideline to meet the team where they were jumping up and down and chanting.

The whistle sounded and the receiving team took the field. Harry Buffington was deep with John Hawley and Phil Andrews on each side of him. The whistle sounded again, and the ball came end over end to Harry. He nestled the ball in his arms and headed straight up the field. He crossed the twenty and headed to his left. He took another two steps, where a white-shirted Torrence player brought him down with a vicious tackle at the twenty-five.

The first offensive unit took the field. Mickey ran quickly to his spot in the huddle. They gathered in their oval with Chad kneeling at the opening in the end. This was it, and Chad was talking.

"Well, gentlemen, this is what we have been waiting for. They will be expecting Billy so let's go with option left on the first go. Ready."

"Break." The sound was deafening again as they came out of the huddle and lined up on the ball.

"Ready. Set. Go."

Tubby snapped the ball and hit out hard. Chad took the ball and put it into Steve's midsection, pulled it out, and headed further down the line to the left. Billy threw a block on the outside linebacker, and they both went down in a pile. Mickey was speeding to his left, conscious of the fact that he may be getting the ball. Chad planted his left foot and turned up field. Just then a Torrence player was going to hit him, and he pitched the ball left to Mickey.

Mickey took the ball in stride and headed up field. The defensive back was aiming at him and then, just like the scrimmage, he avoided him, moved to the middle and made several other players miss badly, and sprinted toward the goal line. He couldn't hear anything but his heart pounding. No one in front of him, and he wasn't looking back. When he crossed the goal line, he was fifteen yards in front of everyone. He turned, let out his air, and was immediately surrounded by black shirts. He couldn't believe it. His first carry, and it was a TD.

The Knights gathered in their oval for the PAT, and Mickey said, "That was for Gary Pearson."

"Man, can you fly," said Billy. "By the time I got to my feet, you were in the end zone."

"That was great ball handling," said Mickey. "I thought that guy had you."

"Okay, you guys," Chad said. "What do you think this is, a mutual admiration society?"

Harry Buffington came in for Mickey, and he headed for the sideline. The cheer he heard sent chills through him. As he reached the area where Coach Barron was all, his teammates were slapping him on the back and congratulating him.

Coach Barron said, "Nice run, Mickey," as he smiled.

Coach Howard came to him and started going over the things he should be looking for on defense. Mickey knew that those points might not hold up, and he had to bear down on defense. A cheer went up as Billy kicked the extra point. Fuller lead 7-0 with less than a minute gone on the clock.

Torrence broke out of the huddle, and Blair moved up under center. He looked directly at Mickey and then the other side. While he was barking the signals, Rich Clover moved slightly to his left so that he would be right in the middle of the off tackle hole. The ball was snapped, and Blair headed Mickey's way. Mickey charged toward Blair and just missed getting hit by the pulling guard. Mickey hit Blair right in the numbers and drove his legs hard. He continued to drive his legs until he and Blair crashed to the ground. The whistle sounded, and Mickey scrambled to his feet. He turned to Blair and said, "That was a Black Knight hit, Mr. Blair."

"Good hit, number 26, but I don't have the ball."

Mickey looked back toward the line of scrimmage and saw Clover and Radcliffe helping the ball carrier back to his feet. "Second and eleven," the announcer said. "Tackle by Clover and Radcliffe."

Mickey smiled and moved back to his spot. He'll know my name before this game is over, he thought.

The next two plays were more of the same, and Torrence had to punt. Billy went back into single safety to receive the punt. Their kicker got off a high spiral, and Billy took it on his own 32. He took a few steps and two Torrence players brought him down. The ball was on the thirty-five-yard line.

The black-shirted Knights gathered in the huddle on the twenty-five.

"Forty-seven, power on the first go," said Chad. "Ready . . ."

"Break," came the chorus. Mickey knew that was him again. What was going on? Billy hadn't run the ball yet.

Chad began the signals. Tubby snapped the ball, and Mickey headed to his left behind Clark and Brown. He snaked through the hole that was there and turned up field. He got five yards and was slammed down by two tacklers.

"Second and five," came the announcer's voice.

In the huddle, Chad again said, "Forty-seven, power on the first go . . . Ready . . . ?"

"Break." Again they called for him to run the ball. What was going on? Same play and almost the same results.

"Third and one," came the announcer again. The Fuller team was moving the ball, and the spectators were calling for another touchdown.

In the huddle, Chad said, "Okay, gentlemen, let's do it again. They are ready for twenty-four counter on the first sound. Ready . . . ?"

"Break."

The black-shirted Knights came out of the huddle and lined up for the snap. As soon as Chad said ready, they hit out at the Torrence line in a sudden crunching sound. To the Torrence team it looked like the same play as the previous two. Billy had taken his step to the left and headed back to his right. Chad put the ball into Mickey's stomach, pulled it out, and gave it to Billy going the other way. Baker and Mason had opened up a hole in the right side, and Billy flew through it. Only one player knew Billy had it, and he stiff-armed him and headed for the goal line. Both safeties were headed to Mickey and saw he didn't have the ball, and it was too late. Billy was sailing to the opposite goal.

Mickey was hit at the line of scrimmage hard and went down. He didn't know what was happening, but he heard the crowd screaming. When he could finally get up, Billy was crossing the goal line. He stood there with the ball, gave it to the official, and the team piled on him. He couldn't believe it, they had scored again. As Mickey headed for the sideline, the band played the fight song.

Harry Buffington was coming in to block again and stopped Mickey.

"I'm in for Billy this time. You are to kick."

Mickey low-fived Billy on the way out and said, "Boy, can you fly."

With that, Billy grinned and headed for the sideline to be greeted the same as Mickey had been.

"Thanks, you guys," Billy said. "But Chad and Mickey made that play work. I didn't think he had the ball when he turned to me."

"Did you hear that?" Coach Rowe said to Coach Howard. "That is the first time I have ever heard Billy credit anyone else but himself during a game."

Coach Rowe went to Billy and said, "Billy, that was some run you just made. When they finally found out you had the ball, it was too late."

A cheer went up in the stands as Mickey's kick went over the goal posts and Fuller led 14-0. The rest of the first quarter was played around the thirty-five-yard lines with both teams exchanging punts. Then in the second quarter with two minutes left, Fuller was fourth and five on their own forty. Mickey was back to punt. Tubby snapped the ball, and it sailed over his outstretched hands. Mickey quickly turned and ran after the ball. He scooped it up in one fluid motion, hoping he could still kick it. No way was he going to kick it with all those white shirts chasing him. He turned to his right, and Torrence's end was getting ready to smash into Mickey when a black blur in the form of Billy Brown erased him from the spot with a thunderous block. The sound of that hit brought the fans to their feet, and Mickey headed up field. The two safeties had him pinned to the sideline, but Mickey stopped and headed the other way. Howie Grant, who had been downfield, wiped out one of the tacklers. Mickey headed the other way, again, and faked out the other one. He got as far as the fourteen-yard line before another white-shirted player knocked him out of bounds.

Mickey didn't get up. He had fallen on the ball and had knocked the wind out of himself. Sparky was over him in a hurry as was Billy.

"Take it easy, Mickey," Billy said.

"What's wrong?" Sparky asked.

"I just got the wind knocked out of me. I'm okay."

Sparky and Billy helped him to his feet, and Sparky was helping him to the sideline.

"I'm okay," Mickey said, yanking his arm from Sparky and trying to go to the huddle.

"Okay, okay," said Sparky. "You have to come out for one play, anyway. That's the rules."

Sparky and Mickey headed for the bench as Phil Andrews was going onto the field to take his place. Fuller ran two plays and gained five yards when Mickey turned to Coach Barron.

"Coach, there is only eighteen seconds left, and I think Billy can kick a field goal from there."

Coach looked at Mickey like he was crazy. Then he turned to Mickey and said, "All right, go in there and call a time-out." He had to stop because they were running another play, and Clark was knocked out of bounds at the fifteen-yard line.

Mickey ran onto the field yelling Andrews name, and they low-fived as they passed. When Mickey got to the huddle, he said, "Coach told me to call a time-out, but the clock is already stopped. If you want the time-out, Chad, check with the bench, but I have the tee. He wants Billy to kick a field goal."

Chad checked the clock, and there was four seconds left. He turned to the official and called a time-out and headed for the bench.

"I told Coach you could make this, Billy, so make it good."
"We do it in practice, but I have never done it in a game."

"It isn't too far. You have the leg. Get it done," said Randy. "There won't be anyone near you."

Chad got to the sideline, and Coach Barron said, "You know, that Daniels is going to make a fine coach when he grows up. He isn't bad right now. I'd probably run another play and missed scoring. Get them together and score three more."

"You got it, Coach," said Chad.

Chad headed back to the huddle, and the fans were screaming for another touchdown. The Knights broke out of the huddle and lined up for a field goal. A hush came over the field. Fuller had never kicked a field goal before, and the fans were stunned. Tubby snapped the ball, and Chad placed it on the tee. There was an ear-smashing roar in Mickey's ears as he blocked one of the defenders. He looked up and high over the crossbar; he spotted the ball sailing through the middle.

The crowd roared again, and Fuller lead 17-0. That was the end of the first half, and the teams headed for the locker room. There was no shouting or yelling. That was taboo to Coach Barron. The cheering came at the end of the game. Never assume you have won until the last second is off the clock.

Mickey, Chad, and Billy were sitting together. The coach had assured them they had won the first half. Now they had to win the second half, too. They hadn't caught on to the Blair giveaway, so that will help. Everything was going well; they just had to keep a high level of intensity. The band was finishing, and they were ready to go back out. They all began to fire up again.

The second half was a little tougher. Torrence scored once and Fuller two more times, making the final score 31-7. Fuller was on the one-yard line when the final horn sounded. They had done so many things right and so few wrong. It was a nice win. Mickey wondered what they would say in the papers when they were thirteen point underdogs and won by twenty-four.

They did their little postgame and practice chant "champs" and headed for the locker room. On the way there, Mickey's father and Mr. Banning fell into step with him.

"That was a mighty fine ball game, Mickey," Mr. Banning said.

"Thank you, sir. They were really tough. They hit harder than we thought. I'm sore all over."

"Son," Mr. Daniels said, "it looked like they adjusted to your option play pretty well. What happened so that you guys couldn't adjust?"

"Well, Dad. Coach Barron didn't want to pass with a seventeen-point lead, and they were playing us for the run. Chad thought we could score through the air, but Coach said no. I don't think we passed once, did we?"

"You didn't have to," Mr. Banning said. "If I had a backfield like yours, I wouldn't pass, either. I think because you had the lead. He wasn't going to give the scouts any other info."

"I have to shower up, Dad. See you at home. I think we are all going to the malt shop."

"Are you taking, Sally?" Mr. Banning asked.

"I haven't asked her, but I am if she will go with me."

"Oh, she will. She is dying for you to ask, but she said she had to ask *you* the last time, and she wasn't going to force herself on you this time."

"Force herself," Mickey stammered. He ran for the showers. When he got there, it was a madhouse. They were all singing, and there were people he didn't even know. Probably some dads, he thought.

Mickey hung up his gear and went to the shower. He felt great. He now felt like he really belonged. Guys gave him pats on the back and said some nice things. His side was a little sore, but he didn't think about it too much. When he came out of the shower, Gary Pearson was sitting in front of his locker.

Mickey wrapped the towel around his waist and walked over to him.

"Thanks, Mickey. Chad told me what you said in the huddle. I wanted a score, but I didn't know you could do it so fast."

"Ha-ha! Thank Chad for that TD. He had guys hanging all over him."

"You know, I don't think I have ever seen two guys as fast as you and Billy in the same backfield before. I wonder what their Coach is saying to their team right now?"

Mickey wondered about that himself. He felt sorry for Gary, but then he wanted to play and all kinds of things happen. When he got hurt and Sparky was taking him to the bench, he thought about Andrews getting his spot. He had to get back in there and secure his position.

Mickey dressed quickly, and he and Chad headed outside. "I'm taking Brenda to the shop, Mickey," Chad said. "What are you planning to do?"

"If Sally is out there, I'm going to ask her to go. You don't mind, do you?"

"No, I'll wait for you at the car."

Mickey looked around for Sally, but he didn't see her. There were tons of kids out there, and Mickey just about gave up looking when a voice behind him said, "Hey, Speedo, can I talk to you?"

It was Billy Brown.

"Sure, Billy. Great game, guy. What's up?"

"You too, Mick. I wanted to talk to you before, but I wasn't too sure what to say until I talked to Sally. She and I have been friends for a couple of years, but we didn't go steady until last year. I'm a year older than her, and I guess I want to play the field, so to speak. I talked to her about it, and she is a nice kid. I guess she just isn't my type, and she is just a kid. That isn't the right word, but I just don't know how to put it. She is too young. Anyway, I heard you liked her and even took her to church. I don't want her to miss out because everyone thinks she is my girl. You know what I mean?"

"Yeah, I do. And, listen, I'm not trying to butt in, either."

"I know that. I just want to make sure she isn't sitting around. They think she is my girl; she isn't. I told her if no one took her to the malt shop, I would, and she could take it from there."

"Believe it or not, Billy, I'm out here looking for her, but I still don't see her."

"Well, believe it or not, she is at the Anderson Maple waiting for you. She said you and Chad have been traveling back and forth together and would meet you there, okay?"

"Great, Billy, see you there."

Mickey sprinted to Chad's car. There, sitting on the fender was a vision. Sally grinned as he came up to the car. No one else was there yet, and Mickey stopped in front of Sally and said breathlessly, "Would you . . ."

"Oh yes, I'd love to. I thought you would never ask." She jumped off the fender and gave him a big hug. She looked up at him, smiling, and gave him a kiss on the lips. Oh. Oh. He was getting weak. Torrence didn't hit him like that. He regained his composure and just held her to him.

She looked up at him and said, "And how is our transfer hero feeling right now?"

Mickey couldn't speak. He just gave her another hug and smiled. Chad and Brenda came to the car, and they all piled in. They had beaten Torrence 31-7, and he had scored twice. Both he and Billy had rushed over 150 yards, and Steve Clark, seventy-five. What amazed Mickey was that Chad had only run the ball six times for thirty-two yards. That is the nature of it. Chad does all the work, and they get all the glory.

When they got to the malt shop, it was so crowded, there were not many chairs. Randy had a table with two chairs, and he waved them over. Mickey held the chair for Sally, but she pushed him down in it and sat on his knee. That is what Chad and Brenda did, too. Now this was too much.

Sally said, "What do you think of our transfer hero?"

Mickey said, "Chad is the hero. He is what makes this team go. You could see that. I'll bet he got tackled as many times as I did, or more."

"You know it is a team," Chad said. "Sally, you had better get used to a boy that is modest. He exemplifies team and modesty. That is why we like him so much."

"Hear! Hear," said Randy. "All for one and one for all. Sally, welcome to the clan. I'm not sure how long you will last, you aren't good looking enough."

They all had a good laugh at that. They finished their malts, and Chad dropped Sally and Mickey off at her house. He walked her to the door. She turned and gave him a big kiss. "I have wanted to do that for a long time."

"Well, me too," said Mickey. "I'll see you tomorrow."

"Okay, Mickey. You were great tonight. I'll get all the play by play from my dad. See you tomorrow."

Chapter 7

The next day, Mickey woke up later than usual and padded into the kitchen. His mother and dad were both there at the table and greeted him with good mornings, and the usual bantering they gave him about being their warrior. Mickey sat down and drank his big glass of orange juice straight down.

His mother busied herself with his breakfast, and his dad said, "Son, you played very well last night. You guys have a great team, just keep it together and you guys can go all the way."

"Thanks, Dad. Coach said it was one of his biggest wins. I'm just glad I got to play."

"Coach Barron told me he was glad you got to play, too. Son, I was really impressed with your team, and you ran better than I thought you could. You broke a lot of tackles that would have brought you down last year."

"It's Mom's milk shakes. I am at 186, now, and maybe I'll get to 190. I didn't weigh myself this morning, but I'll bet I lost five pounds last night."

"Your team was in a lot better shape than Torrence. You could tell that in the fourth quarter, when you were marching down the field."

"I didn't get tired at all, until after the game. Maybe that is because it is so exciting to be winning. I never had time to think how tired I was."

"That Chad Anderson is the best high school quarterback I have ever seen."

"You got that right, Dad. He only had thirty-two yards last night."

"That shows how good he is. All the yardage came after his fakes. That's a good QB."

The doorbell rang, and Mrs. Daniels went to the door. Mickey had his back to the hallway where his mother went, and she returned with Sally. Sally walked up behind Mickey and kissed him on the forehead.

Startled, Mickey straightened up and his mouth fell open. "Good morning, hero," she said.

"Oh, hi, Sally." He jumped up and pulled the fourth chair out for her to sit in. Sally had on her letter sweater with the big black F in the middle.

"All the kids are getting together at the park at noon and are having hotdogs and soda. I wasn't sure if you knew about it, so I thought I would remind you. Are you going?"

"I didn't know about it, Sally, but sure, I'll go. What do I have to take?"

"Good, then you are taking me, okay?"

"Sure, but what all do I need?"

"I have everything ready this time. You can buy the next time."

Mickey asked his dad for the car, but Sally said she wanted to walk. It wasn't very far, and it was a beautiful day. Sally kissed him on the cheek and ran out to the front door. "See you about eleven thirty, okay?"

"I'll be there."

Mickey got up to go to his room, and he looked at his parents. They were both sitting there with their arms crossed and huge smiles on their faces. He felt so very good. He went to the bathroom and got on the scale. It read 185. He only lost one pound. He was so happy he had gained the weight. He didn't feel any different, but he did know that it did make a difference. His legs were so much stronger, too.

Mickey cleaned himself up and combed his short hair. The thought of how lucky he was kept running through his mind. It was like a fairy tale. He was even going on a picnic with the prettiest girl in town. Plus, he was the starting halfback on the Fuller football team and had scored two touchdowns. What more could he ask?

His dad came into the bedroom and said, "You know, that Sally Banning is a real knockout. I know I don't have to tell you this but I'm going to anyway. You treat her nice, okay? Remember your manners."

"Hey, Dad, I'm not a kid anymore and I like her, too. Have you ever seen me treat anyone badly? Besides, I have the greatest role model right here in my house."

"Thanks, Mickey. All I know is that you belted her once already and that isn't like you, either."

"Aw, come on, Dad, that is water over the dam. I really like her. I think I would fight anyone that treated her badly, myself."

"Well, that's good. Everything is going so good that I don't want anything rocking the boat."

"Nothing is going to go wrong if I can help it."

His dad left the room, and Mickey hurried and made his bed and put his dirty clothes in the hamper. He got out a light sweater and slipped it over his head. He grabbed his *Sports Illustrated* and sat down in the living room and began to read. Before he knew it, his mother was yelling, "Mickey, it's twenty-five after eleven."

"Thanks, Mom." He put his magazine away, checked his hair in the mirror by the door, and headed outside. His mother met him there with another big glass of orange juice. She held it out for him, and he said, "Mom, there is no practice or game today."

"I know, honey, but it has been good luck since August and I don't want anything going wrong now."

"Cut it out, Mom. I'm going to tell Sally what a big thing you and Dad are making out of Sally and me."

"You won't either, young man. It would embarrass you more than it would us. We can get away with things like that. Now go and have fun."

"See you later, Mom," Mickey said as he wiped the last of the orange juice off his mouth with the back of his hand. He loved OJ, and if that was what was working, he would drink the whole pitcher. He headed for Sally's house, humming the Fuller's fight song.

Mickey and Sally walked to the park, hand in hand, chatting about the game and how they played. They talked about things at school and some of the events that would be coming up. When they finally arrived at the park, Mickey had forgotten about football. He was thinking about Sally.

The afternoon was spent with most of the athletes eating as much as they could and the girls waiting on them. Mickey thought how nice it would be to be married to Sally and her waiting on him all the time. Then his mind drifted again. Heck, she shouldn't be waiting on him; he should be waiting on her. Mickey jumped up from his spot on the ground with the other guys and joined Sally, where she was busily packing up things she had brought.

"Can I help?" he asked.

"No, it's all ready. Are you ready to go?"

"Sure, let me get my sweater."

Mickey walked back, got his sweater, and said walking away, "See you guys later. It was fun."

"See you, Mickey," Randy said. "Don't get lost on the way home."

That brought a chuckle to them all, and Sally and he headed home. He said to Sally, "Don't ever let me do that again. You aren't a waitress. I should be waiting on you."

"It is okay. It is us girls' way of showing you that what you do for our school is appreciated. Besides, I like waiting on you."

As they were walking, he told himself he was the lucky one. The town of Fuller is great. The kids were the best, his parents were supportive, and the school was a nice place. His parents liked it here—his dad liked his job, and his mother was really into her boy's being happy. He was playing football on the first team, and he was dating a wonderful and beautiful girl. There it was. He had the best of it.

All the following week they were preparing for Bradon. It would be a league game, and they were playing away. Coach Barron had put in several new plays and one was a screen pass. It depended which side it went to if he or Billy was to be the receiver. Each time they ran it in practice, it gained twenty or more yards. Chad did a great job setting it up.

At the Thursday night practice, Sparky was going around handing out the gold footballs for their helmets. They all got one for the win, and Mickey had earned five all together. If this kept up, he might not have enough room on his helmet. Billy had six, Chad five, and so on, and they were all eager to put them on.

The practice went smoothly, and they did their sprints at the end of practice. Coach gathered them at the center of the field and said, "Gentlemen, tomorrow night we open our league schedule with Bradon. They aren't the best team in the league, but they are a good football team. Any team can beat another team on any given night, remember that. We aren't rated this week, and we have something to prove. I won't pour on the score if we are up big, so we have to do everything right and show the sportswriters that we have a great team. We were a little sloppy on our defensive moves, and we *must* keep Bradon from scoring. Now shower up and hit the books for Friday's exams."

The team shouted and sprinted for the gate. They broke into the school fight song and sang it all the way to the school. As Mickey jogged, he passed Sally and said, "Want to go to the malt shop?"

"Sure, Mickey. Why do you think I am hanging around?"

"See you in a few minutes."

He went into the locker room, humming the fight song. He was amazed at how fast he had learned it, and it was a catchy tune. He hung up his gear, showered, and was sitting in front of his locker, putting on his shoes when Gary Pearson came up and sat down.

"Mickey, I asked you to get me a TD last week, and my leg doesn't seem to be getting better, so this week I want a win, okay? Chad says we could hold this team to minus yardage, right, Chad?"

"They have a good back in Allison, but they don't seem to have much of a line that I could see on film. Coach says we are going to play it close to the vest so Avon won't pick up too much about us. They will have their scouts there, but all they will see is a well-oiled machine. We should win with no mistakes."

"Okay then," said Gary, "I want a TD from all four of the backs."

"Wow!" said Chad, "Now you have given us a real challenge. It all depends on the situations. So it will be pure luck if you get your wish."

"Not with you guys on the field. It's up to Bradon to keep me from getting my wish. I feel sorry for them."

Mickey, Chad, and Randy headed out together, and there waiting for them were Sally, Brenda, and Sue. Mickey grinned when he saw Sally and took her arm and headed for the Anderson Maple. The night was warm with a little breeze, and as they walked, he could smell her perfume. He put his nose under her ear and said, "Mmmmm!" The smell of her again sent chills down his back.

They were all kidding each other and talking about the upcoming game and how much more relaxed they were because this team wasn't as tough. Chad reminded them that that is when you get knocked off. When they reached the car under the maple, Ron Richmond from the *Daily News* was there.

"Hello, fellows. Coach Barron didn't want me in the locker room but said I could talk to you out here. He didn't want any favoritism shown but said you would show up under this tree. He was right. Will Billy Brown be out here?"

"No," said Chad. "He has already gone. By now he is in Dalton. His girlfriend lives over there, or the girl he is dating now is from Dalton."

"No matter, I just want to ask a few questions. I had your game last week, and you guys are one fine football team. I told my boss about you, and he registered his vote for you in the state rankings, so they will hear about you from now on. All you have to do is keep winning. Dalton won big last week, and what I want to know is if you think the league will depend on your game with Dalton?"

"I don't know if it will or not," said Chad, "but we are going to win all our games. The rest is up to Dalton."

"You are Mickey Daniels, aren't you?"

Mickey nodded his head and wondered what he was going to ask him. He had remembered what Coach had said the first time about giving something for the other team to use, so he had to be careful what he says.

"You are new to the team this year, right? Was it hard breaking into the lineup, and how do you like the teams' chances this year?"

"I didn't break into the lineup. Gary Pearson hurt his leg. I was on the second team at the time. As for the team, they are great guys, and we all like each other. This team does so many things together, and we have great coaches who care about us. I came from Moorhead, and it was so much bigger, but this team is so much fun to be with. Our chances? Chad says we are going all the way, and when the best quarterback in the state tells you something, then you better believe it."

"That is a good response. How do you think you will do tomorrow night?"

"Chad said we are going all the way," Randy said, "so that means we are going to win. Keep your eye on the ball this week, Mr. Richmond, or you will miss most of the game. We have Houdini in the backfield."

They all chuckled and piled in the car. As they headed for the shop, Chad said, "I wish you guys would quit building me up like that."

"Why not?" Randy asked. "It's true, and you never seem to get any of the glory."

"That isn't important. You guys are my team, and if you believe in me, that is all that matters."

"Well, we believe in you," Mickey said. "I have believed in you since that first day in my side yard."

Friday was a day of tests for Mickey, and he could keep his mind off football until the bell rang to change classes. He and Sally ate lunch together, and Mickey was very quiet. He was thinking football, and Sally knew it but she said, "Is there anything wrong, Mickey?"

"No, I was just thinking about tonight. I sure hope the guys aren't over confident."

"I don't think they will be. Look around the lunchroom. All the players look like they are in a trance. A girl might as well stay away from their guy until after the game. You don't even know we are here."

"Oh, I know you are here all right. I was just thinking about tonight."

"That's what I mean. Your mind is on the game, and you don't have time for us."

"I like being with you, Sally. I don't know how to say this, but it makes me feel real good to just be with you. I would be a nervous wreck if I was sitting with the guys, and we were all talking football. I just like to think of things I have to do, and I would rather do that with you here."

"Okay, Mickey. That's nice. I understand, but it is just like being a coach's wife. I bet they never talk to their husband on game day."

"You're probably right." His mind drifted back to football.

Bradon had a well-coached team, but their talent wasn't as good as Fuller's. Both teams were loosening up at their end of the field, and Mickey was looking for number 22. Allison wasn't all that big, he thought, same size as me. No matter, they had to stop him and make no mistakes.

Bradon won the toss and elected to receive. They returned the kickoff to the twenty-four-yard line. As the defense was going onto the field, Mickey was more nervous than he thought he would be. They only had a week to get ready for them instead of the four they had for Torrence. Before Mickey had another thought, Bradon was running a play. They were heading right at him with a blocker, and Mickey sidestepped him and threw his body right at the numbers of the runner. At the same time, Cliff Martin hit the runner, too. It was a terrible sound, and he knew something had to give. As they unpiled, the Bradon's runner didn't get up. It was number 22. Mickey wasn't nervous anymore, either. His adrenalin was really flowing.

The Bradon's trainer came out and, several minutes later, they were helping Don Allison off the field. Two plays later, Bradon punted and Fuller took over at their own forty-one-yard line. Fuller ran six plays with Clark, Brown, and Daniels alternating. From the five-yard line, Clark took two tacklers into the end zone. Brown converted the point after and Fuller led 7-0.

After Fuller's kickoff, Bradon started on their own twenty-five with what they thought would be a surprise pass, but when the back went into motion, Mickey knew they were going to throw to him in the flat. He hung back a little and let the quarterback think he was open. When he cocked his arm to throw, Mickey raced in front of the motion man and intercepted the ball. It was a quick twenty-eight-yard sprint for Mickey for the touchdown and, after his own kick, Fuller led 14-0. They still had more than half of the first quarter to go.

Bradon ran three plays after the ensuing kickoff and punted to Billy Brown, which he took at his own forty-five and raced toward the goal. Picking up several key blocks and stiff-arming the last man, he raced into the end zone with their third TD. Billy made the conversion kick and Fuller led 21-0. Mickey's kickoff went to the ten-yard line, and the Bradon's player fumbled the ball, picked it up, and was hit so hard he fumbled again. Phil Andrews fell on the ball at the fifteen-yard line, and Fuller was on offense again.

In the huddle, Chad said, "I thought we would be a little down after Torrence, but you guys are amazing. Let's get one of you another score. You know if we do, though, we may be done for a while. Okay, let's go with option right on the first sound. Ready?"

"Break."

They came to the line, knowing Billy was getting the pitch from Chad. Mickey just wanted to throw a good block.

"Ready." The ball was snapped, and Chad put the ball in Clark's stomach. He pulled it out as Clark was getting tackled and headed to his right. He got to the end, and he was in his pitch line, so he faked to Billy and headed for the goal. Mickey hit the safety and drove him to the ground. Chad went into the end zone, untouched.

In the huddle for the point after, Chad said, "Wow! Did you kiss that safety with a sweet block? I think he thinks he was hit by a truck."

"It was great doing something for you for a change. I didn't see it, but it must have been a great fake," said Mickey.

"I thought I was getting the ball," said Billy. "You faked me out, too." The kick by Mickey was good, and it was 28-0 with six minutes to go in the first quarter.

Coach Barron put in the second team, and the Fuller fans were cheering loudly. It was a great feeling. At the half, Fuller was leading 35-0, and the starting team opened the second half. They ran an option play to the left, and Mickey ran sixty-five yards, zigzagging through the secondary. It was 42-0, and Coach replaced the starters.

After the game, Coach Barron met them in the locker room and said, "Every game won't be that easy. I don't know if they were that bad or we are that good, but this I will say, you are fun to watch and coach." A cheer went up, and Coach Barron spoke again. "We have Avon next, and after your get-together at the park tomorrow, I would like you to come to the school at four and watch some film with the coaches. Maybe we can pick something up like we did with Torrence. You played well and deserved to win. Nice going."

They cheered again and headed for the showers. Mickey knew the people outside could hear them singing the fight song. When Mickey left the locker room, he met Sally and told her about the film session the next day. He explained why and wasn't sure how long he would be there because he wanted to be with her.

She hugged his arm, and they walked to the car where Chad was waiting. They went to the shop, and then Chad dropped them off at Sally's house. They sat on her front steps, and he told her how good he felt. Things were so much fun right now. He was wondering how she felt about things so he asked.

"Well, Mickey," she said, "this is the best time of my life. Things are so good I can't believe it. Mom and Dad are so happy that you and I are going together. Well, me too."

"Listen, Sally, and if this is wrong or anything, just tell me, but I have to tell you this. I really think I am falling in love with you."

"Mickey, I . . ."

"No, let me finish." He looked her in the eyes, and she was crying. "Gee, don't cry, Sally. I'm sorry, but I don't know what to do. I just love the way you make me feel, the way you treat my parents and the way I feel when I am with you and around people."

"Mickey, I have wanted to hear that since the day you and your dad came to the house. You make me feel the same way. I am so proud of you, and you are the first boy who treats me like you do. Everyone else sees me for something else. Mickey, I love you, too. Please make this last forever. I never dreamed I could feel this way."

"Sally, stop crying or you are going to make me cry. My dad and mom think you are tops, and Dad even threatened me about being nice to you."

"You're kidding! Your dad threatened you?"

"Yep, he said if I treated you badly, he would knock my block off."

"He is so cute. My parents really like your parents. Well, come on and give me a kiss. You have to get home or you will be in trouble.

"I would like to sit here all night with you, but you're right, I have to go." They kissed and held onto each other a little longer, and he got up and jogged home, thinking what a wonderful feeling it was to tell her he loved her. As he approached the house, his mom and dad were there on their front steps to meet him. Something was wrong. They started asking him questions.

"What are all the questions for? What is so important that you have to quiz me outside?" Mickey asked.

"Well," his father began, "there is a rumor that Coach Barron is going to quit after this season, and Mr. Banning said to ask the players what they had heard. I just wondered if there was anything wrong with the team, or the coach, or is there some other reason."

"Gosh, Dad. I haven't heard anything like that at all. Where did you hear this?"

"I heard it at the store so I asked Fred Banning. Everything is going so good and you look like you can be real good next year, too. I just hate to see the team lose a guy like him because you all seem to like him so well."

"I do, Dad. I'll ask some of the guys tomorrow."

Mickey and his parents went into the house, and Mickey headed for the kitchen. There on the table was his milk shake. He told his mother he always got a shake at the shop, but she made them anyway. He took the shake and headed for the living room. He thought he would listen to the TV and see how some of the other teams had done. He slumped into the big-stuffed chair and settled back with his shake. A movie was just ending, and his mother joined him because she liked to hear the weather report.

Sports came on and the announcer started with the scores. Dalton beat Cade City 30-6. Cade City was supposed to be real good, too. They moved on with the other scores, and there was Fuller, 42-0. When he had finished all the scores, he said, "Looks as if Dalton and Fuller are the teams to be reckoned with. They should make the ratings this week."

Mickey looked at his mother, and she was smiling. He went to his bedroom, quickly got ready for bed, and jumped in. He was hoping both teams would be undefeated when they met.

Sally and Mickey had gone to the park, and they chatted about the game and the upcoming game with Avon. Several of the players had heard the rumor, too, but didn't know anything else. They would just have to wait and see. Mickey was lying in the grass with Sally laying perpendicular to him with the back of her head on his stomach.

"I hope we can do things like this forever," she said.

"Me too. This is the life, eh?"

Sally jumped up and helped the other girls clean up, and the boys got in the cars and headed for school. Chad left his car for Brenda, and they went five and six to a car to school.

They assembled in the film room, where they had watched films before. They were told to watch all the positions that would affect each one of them and that would help. They made comments all through the film about all sorts of things.

Mickey was interested in their offensive plays. He wasn't worried about running the ball. What he was worried about was what they did when they *had* the ball. Coach noticed that they usually ran the fullback on first down. The projector was running in slow motion, and Randy said, "Coach, when they are in the 5-3 defense, the tackles pinch inside, and when they are in their 5-4, they move outside."

"Good point, Randy," Coach Barron said. "Chad, if that holds true to form, we will use an audible at the line."

That meant that Chad could change the play after they set their defense. The film continued for another ten minutes when Chad said, "Coach, I'm not sure if it has been consistent through the whole film, but they never run to the split end side unless they have a back in motion to that side. See, on the play they are running right now, the split end is right. They are going to run left. No! No, wait a minute, here comes the half in motion to the right. They are running right."

They were all watching the screen, and as soon as the ball was snapped, the quarterback quick-pitched to the right, and the split end and the motion man came crashing back to block. Coach Barron backed the film up, and they watched the play again. The film continued, and the next several plays were the same. Chad picked up a few things, and they watched for another fifteen minutes.

Coach Barron stopped the film and said, "Gentlemen, I am going to call State, and see if they want you to analyze their films. You guys are too much."

"Coach, they can't afford us," Randy said.

They all laughed, and Coach Barron said, "We will watch this again Monday after practice. That's all for now, and thank you for taking the time away from your friends. Coach Rowe says there has to be twenty girls in the gym waiting for you lover boys."

"It's those girls that inspire us, Coach," Randy said. "You ought to have them waiting in the end zone and we would get there a lot quicker." They all laughed and started filing out.

"Chad, Billy, and Randy, stick here for a moment, will you?" Coach asked. The room cleared and the three boys remained behind. Coach was sitting on the film desk and waited for the boys to reseat themselves in front of him. They sat down and looked at him expectantly.

"There is a rumor going around that I am done here after this season. I want you to know that it isn't true, and I haven't ever talked about anything like that to anyone. I know the AD at Dalton has said that I was, and it is probably something to get us shook up. You are the captains. Make sure the team knows what I just said and that I love coaching here and would be nuts to leave. This should come from you guys. Any questions?"

"You answered the big one, Coach," said Chad. "We weren't sure, but Mickey said it was going around the stands last night."

"I know, that is why I had to say something today. My phone has been ringing off the hook all morning and that darned sportswriter called two or three times. Well, that's all I have. See you Monday."

The three boys climbed out of their seats and headed outside. When they got there, the whole team was waiting for them with all the girls who had been waiting.

"Coach says the rumor is hogwash, you guys," Randy yelled. A *big* cheer went up, and Coach looked out the door.

"We're number one champs. We're number one champs." The sound echoed off the building and almost shook the glass. Coach Barron grinned and thought they probably could hear them all the way in town.

The news that Coach gave them made them closer as a team. That week's practices seemed like a dream. Gary Pearson had his leg in a cast now to prevent further damage. He was always on the practice field, yelling encouraging things. Too bad he couldn't play; he was a great guy.

It was game night, and Avon was the opponent. Mickey had so much on his mind. Coach Barron's voice brought him out of his trance. The familiar, "Let's go," fired him up. The game was starting with them receiving the kickoff. The ball was in the air and heading for Billy. They ran straight ahead, and Mickey hit the first dark shirt, and the crowd gasped. Billy swerved and ran over the next Avon player, and he was on his way to the goal line. Wow, that was too easy.

And that is the way the game went. Fuller had routed the Avon Bulldogs 45-0. The game was fast because they had a running clock after halftime. Billy had scored three times and kicked a field goal, while Mickey had scored twice and kicked four extra points. Chad had run the team like a general, changing plays at the line that totally confused Avon. Fuller's offense was terrific, but their defense was getting better, too.

Chapter 8

The next three games were more of the same. Bluffton fell 28-0; Kensington 42-13; and Howard 52-6. They were on a roll, and all was good for the knights. The kids were in the malt shop and having a good time. Randy was entertaining everyone with his comic remarks. Suddenly Chad said, "We are six, and oh, three to go."

"You're a poet," Randy said. They laughed and then it sunk in. They were 6-0 with Cade City up next. If they all did their jobs with no mistakes, this could be a breather, Mickey thought. No, no, I can't think that way. Every game is a big game. He and Sally got up, and Mickey told them they wanted to walk.

It was ten blocks, but the nights were going to start getting a little cooler. Mickey grasped Sally's hand and squeezed. "I never dreamed all this could happen to me in such a short time. The best part is that I met you. Sally, I'm not sure I deserve all this."

"Mickey, I'm not sure I do, either, and if it is a dream, please don't wake me." She pulled him to a stop and lifted her face to him to be kissed. He marveled at her beauty and also at himself. He had been so shy when he was at Moorhead. I guess I am growing up, he thought. He took her in his arms and kissed her. He quickly stopped and looked around, embarrassed. He was one happy boy.

They continued to walk home holding hands, swinging them to and fro. Happy wasn't a word big enough for how he felt. They got to Sally's house, and they made plans to go to the park. He kissed her goodnight and went home.

Cade City was their next opponent, and the coaches were confident they were ready. Their practices had been crisp, and they even added a few new plays. The guys were having a ball, and they couldn't wait for Friday night. When it finally got here and they were boarding the bus, there was an electricity that filled the air. Coach Barron got on the bus and said, "We have a thirty-minute ride to Cade City. Spend it thinking about your assignments. Our last two games are at home and that should help. This is Cade City's homecoming. They will be jacked up. Just do your job, and we can put a damper on their dance tonight."

And they certainly did their job. Cade City fell 28-0 with Billy scoring three times and Chad once on a seventy-five-yard keeper off the option. The ride home was singing the fight song about every five minutes. Then Chad yelled, "seven, and oh, with two to go." They rocked the bus, and Coach was worried they were going to tip over.

When they pulled into the parking lot, there was a big crowd there. The band had gotten there while they were showering at Cade City, and they played the fight song as they got off the bus. They felt like celebrities. Sally rushed up to Mickey and gave him a hug, as many of the other girls did to their guys. Mickey grabbed his bag and said, "Let's go to the shop and get a shake."

"Right on, Speedo," Billy said.

"I should be calling you Speedo. I can still see all those guys chasing you. You made them look so bad."

"He had one of their wallets," Randy said. They all laughed and headed for the cars.

Two games left. Melvindale was homecoming for Fuller, and Brenda and Sue were senior candidates, and Sally was the junior rep. Three good-looking girls, too bad they all can't be the queen, Mickey thought. Sally will be the queen next year for sure.

When they got to the shop, Ron Richmond was there waiting for them. "Hi, guys. Nice job. Did you hear that Dalton won 56-0?"

"No," said Chad. "We just take care of our end. Those were some pretty nice things you said about our team. Thanks a lot."

"Well, you are the team that I am covering, even though I am from Dalton. Your team is every bit as good as theirs. I'm not sure they know how good you are. I know they have watched film on you, but they don't hear the pads cracking."

"They will in two weeks," Randy said.

"Careful, now," said Chad. "Remember, no bulletin board info for Dalton."

"Don't worry, guys," said Richmond. "I wouldn't do that to you. Those guys from Dalton are so darn cocky and braggarts. I'm not sure there is anyone on that team I like, even the coach. They think they are going to crush you."

"Well, let them think that way," said Mickey. "We are a good team, and we do our talking on the field."

"That's for sure," Richmond said. "Keep it up. You guys give me so much to write about that they keep trying to cut my articles down. This has been a fun season to be a reporter."

"Well, we have to get our shake and get home, Mr. Richmond," said Chad.

"Good luck this Friday," he said.

They went in, got their shakes, and headed home. Mickey told Sally he was really tired so he wanted to get some sleep before they went to the park the next day. She felt the same way so they kissed goodnight, and Mickey went home to bed.

Their day at the park was great. The three coaches showed up, and the guys were excited. They had brought ice cream bars for everyone. The girls were flitting about and waiting on the coaches like they were kings. As the coaches were leaving, Coach Howard said, "Now I know why you guys come here every Saturday. These girls treat you like royalty."

Off they went and the girls were cleaning up. Mickey knew exactly what Coach Howard meant. He felt like that, anyway. It was almost like being married.

Melvindale provided Fuller with quite a challenge. They were a passing team, and Fuller hadn't seen too much of that so far. Mickey had told the coaches in their last meeting that if Fuller could keep control of the ball, they couldn't be throwing it. So right he was, and the fact that Fuller had put Chad and Billy both in the secondary for the last two games would help.

This was going to be a pretty busy week, Mickey thought. He wondered what homecoming would be like in a smaller town. It sure was a big thing in Moorhead with all the alums coming back. This was going to be much different because he didn't know any of the past or its history. He would know soon enough.

At Monday's practice, coach gathered the team together and told them about some things he knew about Melvindale and how they were going to defend this team. Then he went into what he called his homecoming speech.

"Boys, this is going to be a big week for all of you. You have to concentrate on your studies, but you have to keep an even balance with that and football. Some of your social life will take a beating because your girls are going to want you to be with them a little more. Just know that there is only so much time for each of those elements. I am sure your girls will understand. You don't need to be up here decorating or any of those frills. Keep your mind on what you have to do. Some of you have girls on the court. Make sure they understand what is at stake. You all can celebrate after the game."

Wow! Mickey thought. He never had to worry about any of that before. Now he has a girl and she is important to him, so he has a few more responsibilities. He made a mental note to talk to her about what Coach said.

The team went out to that afternoon practice and began to loosen up. Gary Pearson was moving about the lines on his crutches and offering encouragement. Mickey knew he really wanted to play because every time he said something his voice would crack. Coach Barron blew his whistle, and the team went into their drills. They had extra drills today because there were more pass defensive drills. They weren't going to let Melvindale hit the long pass.

The week went pretty fast, and the pregame assembly for the queen was spectacular. Each girl was ushered into the gym by the boy of her choice. Every candidate this year was ushered in by a football player, even the freshman and sophomore court members. The boys all wore a black varsity sweater with the big F on the front. However, Mickey and the two younger boys didn't have a letter on the front. Chad had gone to the coach and asked if Mickey could wear a sweater with an F on it, but Mickey told him that he wasn't any better than anyone else and he would earn his F.

When Sally heard about the sweater deal, she went to Mickey and said, "Mickey, you always seem to say the right thing. Coach Barron was so proud of you when you said you had to earn your right to wear the F on your sweater."

"It's no big deal to me, Sally. I just don't want to make you look bad. All the other upperclassmen will have a letter on their sweater. Anyway, they won't be looking at me with you on my arm."

"Oh, Mickey. See, you always say the right thing. Isn't all this fun?"

"It sure is, but Coach Barron doesn't want us to get caught up in the festivities. Heck, I won't even get to see you on the field in your pretty dress. I hope your mother will take some movies of you and your dad walking across the field."

"She said she would." Then Sally laughed and told him, "Mom said she would be so nervous that the camera would look like it was on a wavy lake." They both chuckled.

As they entered the gym, the kids were all cheering. When Sally's name was announced with Mickey as her escort, a feeling of great pride rushed through Mickey. Sally was wearing her cheerleading uniform and, as Mickey looked down at her, had a huge grin on her face. She looked up at him and winked.

Mickey felt like he had jelly in his shoes. They stood in front of the student body as the senior candidates were brought in, and the atmosphere was electric. He had never been through anything like this. Now he knew what Coach Barron meant when he told them not to get caught up in the festivities. He sure wasn't thinking football right now.

The Thursday night pregame practice was coming to a close, and Coach gathered the team together. They were all waiting for him to speak, and no one was saying anything. Coach Howard came forward and said, "Coach, can I say a few words?"

"Sure, Coach Howard."

"Guys, I have been coaching almost twenty years now and I have never been through a season like this one. Tomorrow, you play a team that wants to beat you real bad. I got an article from their home newspaper, and their captain said they would beat you because you are looking to Dalton and not thinking about them. Make sure that isn't true because that is when the roof falls in. You are definitely ready, so just take it to them. Thanks, Coach."

"Well, guys, Coach just took my speech so get through those tests tomorrow and get the job done against Melvindale."

They all hustled to the fifty-yard line, did their ten sprints, and headed for the shower, singing the fight song. After showering, they went to the malt shop, where Randy was holding court with his comedy. Mickey wished he could be a little like that and then he wouldn't be so wound up worrying about things. One of the younger boys came over to their table and said that a reporter was outside and wanted to talk to the guys at the table. They all got up and went outside, even the girls.

Ron Richmond was waiting for them. Chad walked up to him and said, "What can we do for you, Mr. Richmond?"

"Thanks for coming out to talk to me. I don't want to bother you, but I just wanted to let you know what Melvindale's captain said about you guys in their paper last night."

"Coach Howard told us about it at practice tonight," Randy said.

"Well, that's good. You guys have been doing so well. I just don't want anything to get in the way of your thinking about them. Their coach seems to think they can pass on you, so just be aware of that, okay?"

Sally said, "They are ready. We have a few things for them, too. It is eleven guys in black jerseys."

"That's the spirit," Ron said. "I sure like covering the games. Good luck tomorrow night."

"Goodnight, Mr. Richmond, and thanks," Chad said. "Gee, Sally, where did that come from?"

"I guess it is from dating a guy that thinks that way. Heck, all you guys think that way."

Friday was here, and the team was finishing dressing and moving outside to go to the field. The excitement of the night was building, and Mickey was still thinking about the defensive assignments when Billy came up behind him and said, "What's on your mind, Speedo?"

"Oh, I was just thinking about their passing game and hoping I was all square with them."

"Listen, we are ready. With Chad and me back there now, we have three of the fastest guys on the team working against their passing. They don't know we made this change. Anyway, if we have the ball the whole time, they can't throw it."

"I hope you're right."

"You know I am and the general will move us down the field on offense."

They headed for the field and went through all their pregame drills. As the three captains came to the group on the sidelines, Randy said, "They won the toss and will receive. That, my friends, is the only thing they are going to win."

The team started jumping up and down and yelling Knights, and then the official blew his whistle. Melvindale took the kickoff back to the fifty-yard line, and Fuller's defense took the field. That runback woke everyone up. Melvindale came out in a strange formation, and Chad yelled to Mickey to watch the flat. Their quarterback took the snap and dropped back to pass, and Mickey saw Fuller's line get through too easy, so he knew it was a screen pass. He sprinted to the side and the quarterback saw him covering his receiver so he turned and tried to throw it out of bounds. Just as he was throwing it, he got hit and the ball went up in the air toward Chad's zone. He outjumped the Melvindale player and headed for the end zone. He got to the thirty-yard line before he was brought down.

Fuller went on offense, and in the huddle, Chad said, "Let's give them a little of their own medicine. We need good fakes in the backfield to make it work. Eighteen option pass on the first sound. Ready."

"Break." The sound was thunderous. No doubt about it, thought Mickey, they were ready. This was to look like the option where he pitched to Billy. Perfect, he thought. They sure will be expecting Brown on the first play.

"Ready." Tubby snapped the ball, and Chad stepped back and stuck the ball in Clark's stomach, pulled it out, and moved down the line to the right. At the same time, Mickey ran right at the safety like he was going to block him and then sprinted right past him. Chad took a couple more steps, stopped and stepped back, and fired a pass to Mickey, who was already ten yards beyond the safety. The crowd was screaming as Mickey pulled the pass in at the twenty and sprinted into the end zone. It was absolute mayhem. The Fuller fans were jumping up and down and screaming, and the Melvindale side was pure silence.

In the huddle for the point after, Chad said, "I hate to admit it, but that was a thing of beauty. Billy, they had two guys sprinting after you when I stopped and threw the ball. They all just stopped and stared."

Billy converted the extra point, and Fuller led 7-0. The Melvindale team took possession of the ball on their own thirty. They tried two passes, which first Billy and then Chad knocked down. The next play, they tried the screen pass again, and Mickey was there to tackle him in his own backfield. They had to punt, and Fuller kept the ball as they marched down the field. The quarter ended, and they changed sides.

In the huddle, Chad said, "Let's try that option pass the other way. They will never expect me to throw it going to my left. Seventeen option pass on the first go. Ready."

"Break."

Tubby again snapped the ball, and Chad put the ball into Steve's stomach, pulled it out, and started down the line to his left, where Mickey was ready for the pitch. Billy did what Mickey had done and then flew by the safety on that side. Chad stopped, stepped back, and fired a perfect spiral to Billy, who was crossing the fifteen-yard line by himself and sprinted into the end zone.

In the huddle for the point after try, Randy said, "I hate to say this, Houdini, but that was a thing of beauty."

Tubby Franklin said, "Boy, this is fun!"

"Oh, shut up and wash your socks," Randy said.

They all laughed, and Chad said, "Our work isn't over yet, guys. Let's take it to them."

They went into halftime leading 14-0, and Coach Barron said, "Don't get overconfident now. We have two quarters to play. Remember all your keys. You are making me look real good, fellas. Thank you."

The second half was basically a war of defenses. Melvindale adjusted pretty well, but Chad was able to score on a keeper play with three minutes left in the game. That pretty much assured a win, but they wanted to keep them scoreless. Melvindale returned the kickoff back to midfield again, but with fourth and nine from the nineteen-yard line and ten seconds left in the game, they decided to try a field goal. It was good, and Fuller acted like they had lost the game.

"Doggone kickers. I hate them," Randy said. "Oh, not you, Billy and Mickey." The sidelines cracked up and the band started playing the fight song. Five seconds left and Cal Radcliffe was in to return the kickoff in Billy's place. He had the stands on their feet as he swept the onside kick up into his hands and sprinted toward the Melvindale goal. They caught him on the four-yard line.

Mickey elbowed Billy in the ribs and said, "If that was you, we would have another six."

"You too, Speedo. What's another six when you already won?"

Homecoming had come and gone. Fuller won 21-3; Brenda was the homecoming queen, and the Black Knights were 8-0. Well, there it was, undefeated going into the Dalton game. Dalton had won, also, so the league was theirs if they won. The papers had said that they both would make the playoffs, win or lose. If they lost, they wouldn't be champs, and they had been chanting that all year. They had studied film on Dalton and there were several keys. They played the same defense that Avon did, so they had a scheme all set up for them. Chad could audible at the line and that would keep them off balance.

Chapter 9

They had just finished the Thursday night practice, and Mickey was walking out to the Anderson Maple in search of Sally. She wasn't there, and he looked all around. He wondered what was wrong, and he was worried. This wasn't like her; she was always there or told him where she would be. Chad started the car and said, "Are you coming?"

Mickey didn't know what to say. He looked around again and started to get in the car. Just then a bright red convertible pulled up next to Chad's car. It was Sally, and she had a big smile on her face. "Going my way, good looking?" she asked with a smile.

Mickey was stunned. Tongue-tied would be a better description. He just ran over to the passenger side and jumped over the door and into the seat.

"See you, lover boy," Chad yelled.

Mickey waved as Chad pulled out of the parking lot. He looked back at Chad, and he had a big smile, too.

"Where did you get this, Sally? Is it your dad's?"

"No, it's mine. My parents said I needed a car and said it was graduation present a year early. Then my mother said I need a nice car to chauffeur my transfer hero around."

"It sure is a nice car. Heck, we only have one car in the whole family."

They headed home, and Sally was going to drop him off at his house, but he said to go right home and he would walk from there. She pulled into the drive, and Mickey got out and opened the door for her. He kissed her on the cheek, said goodnight, and ran home.

When Sally got to the door, Mr. Banning said, "He sure is a polite young man." Sally nodded and smiled and went inside. Mr. Banning watched Mickey jog home and was happy his daughter was dating a boy as nice as Mickey.

It was Friday and the school had just finished the pep rally. Many of the town folks were there. The gym had been packed. The team headed for the lunchroom for the pregame meal. Not much was being said. They were focused. They finished the meal and went to the locker room for equipment check. There on the bench in front of every locker was a brand-new black jersey and black pants with gold stripes. The Boosters had purchased them. The team was buzzing about them, and Randy said, "Do you think we should jinx ourselves and wear this new stuff?"

"It isn't the uniform," Chad said, "it's what we put in them."

With that they all picked their jerseys up and looked at them. They had their names across the back and "Knights" across the front over the number. Now they were really the Black Knights. The next forty-five minutes passed quickly, and they were in front of the chalkboard with Coach Barron talking.

"This is what we have been waiting for. It is the Dalton game and all the marbles are on the line. I don't need to go over anything, just do your job and we will be fine. You seniors, this is your last Dalton game. We won't even play them in the playoffs because they are one division up, so get it done tonight. The ratings are in, Dalton is number two and we are number six. Play like you are number one. I love you guys. Let's get outside."

They went through their pregame routine, and everything went smoothly. The stands were already full, and people were two and three deep around the fence and still coming in. Mickey was glad they were playing at home. He had seen

Dalton's stadium, but he liked Fuller's better. Two minutes before kickoff and Fuller was to receive.

The receiving team was on the field, and the tension was high. Dalton kicked off, and the ball went to Mickey. Here we go, he thought. He caught the ball, and following Billy, fought back to their own forty-one. They went to the huddle, where Tubby was standing with his arm up. Chad kneeled in the open end and said, "Nice night for a football game, gentlemen. Let's show these guys how to play this game. Twenty-four, power on the first sound. Ready . . ."

"Break." The sound was startling to Mickey even now and knew it had to have some effect on Dalton. The linemen got into their position. Chad moved up under center and . . .

"Ready." Fuller shot off the ball quickly, catching Dalton off guard. Randy and Howie opened a hole you could drive a truck through. Mickey hit the hole first and looked for any white shirt he could find. He knew Billy was right behind him so he had to move fast. The backer moved toward him, and he put his helmet, shoulders, and forearms into his numbers. The defender flew to the side, and Mickey stumbled but kept his feet. Billy was at his side, and they both headed downfield. Mickey threw his body at the safety, and they both went down in a pile. Billy jumped the two players and continued on for another ten yards before he was brought down from the side.

They returned to the huddle, and the announcer's voice said, "First down, Fuller. That was a twenty-six-yard run by Brown. Ball is on the Dalton 33."

"Nice blocking, you guys. You're making this look easy," said Billy.

"Quiet," said Chad. "Option right on the first go. Ready . . ."
"Break."

Again they lined up. Chad began calling the signals. "Ready. Set. Go."

The team hit out quickly, and Chad stepped back, put the ball into Clark's stomach, pulled it out, and continued down the line to the right. He started to pitch the ball to Billy, but then he planted his right foot, turned and headed up the field. He eluded two or three tacklers and was knocked out of bounds at the thirteen-yard line. Chad had gained twenty more yards.

They had Dalton on the ropes, and the game just started. In the huddle, Chad called the option right again, and they broke the huddle and lined up. Dalton shifted their defense into a 5-4 setup, so Chad called an audible. "Black 44. Black 44."

Chad knew that was him. A straight dive play. Tubby snapped the ball, and Mickey sprinted straight ahead. Chad stepped quickly to his right and gave Mickey the ball. He flew through the line and had only the safety to beat. He ran right at him and faked left and then moved to his right, leaving the safety off balance and grabbing air. He sprinted into the end zone, untouched. The home crowd went wild, and the band was playing the fight song.

Mickey flipped the ball to the official and headed for the sideline. This is getting to be old hat, he thought. He had felt like jumping over the goal posts the first time he scored and now he expected to score that easily. It wasn't old hat to the team. They lifted him up and spun him around. He went over to Coach Rowe and said, "Chad called an audible, and they didn't know what hit them."

"Chad is the general," Coach Rowe said. "He will be tough to replace next year. They don't come along like him very often."

"You can say that, again," said Mickey.

Billy kicked the extra point and Fuller led 7-0. Fuller kicked off and Dalton had the ball on their own seventeen. Fuller's defense was on the field, and they were ready. Dalton went into a double wing and had a split end, too. No way, they were going to run, thought Mickey. Only one back and that wasn't going to work against their setup. When the ball was snapped, he made a quick pass to the split end, and Mickey was there when he tried to catch it. He hit him and the ball flew up in the air, and Billy made a diving interception on the twenty-five. It was Fuller's ball, and the crowd was screaming.

The offense set up on Tubby again, and Chad kneeled. "Coach is going to kill me, but let's run that new play, the hook and ladder right. Mickey, just take your three steps and turn because the ball will be in your face. On the first sound, ready . . ."

"Break."

They lined up, and Mickey was just to right of the right end. Coach Barron started waving his arms and yelling like mad, but Chad barked out, "Ready."

Tubby snapped the ball, and Chad turned quickly and threw where Mickey was going to be. Mickey turned and the ball was inches from his helmet, but he caught the ball. Billy was sweeping to the right, and Mickey took a step to his right away from Billy, turned back, and pitched it out to him. Billy caught it in stride and sprinted into the end zone, untouched. The stands were a madhouse. Mickey headed for the sideline but was called back to kick, and Billy left. The kick was good and Fuller led 14-0.

It looked like Coach Barron was eating his head set. Mickey wasn't sure if he was happy or angry. Coach Barron turned to Coach Howard and said, "I don't think they need us tonight. This is just unbelievable. Who would have thought this could happen?"

Fuller kicked off, and the Dalton runner brought the ball all the way back to the Fuller's forty-seven-yard line. That woke the Fuller players up and made them know this was going to be a game. As they were lining up for the first play, a Dalton player came running onto the field. Mickey recognized him as the second team quarterback, but their regular quarterback stayed in the game. Trick play, Mickey thought. The new player lined up in front of Mickey, and he was fidgeting a little and knew he must be getting the ball. When the ball was snapped, the back started to turn toward the other quarterback, and Mickey sprinted to where he thought the ball would be. The quarterback turned and threw the ball without looking or he would have seen Mickey moving into position.

Mickey sprinted straight ahead, and he caught the ball as if it was intended for him. He caught it at the fifty and sprinted straight for the goal line. He was twenty-five yards ahead of anyone and the stands erupted into a frenzy. The cheering and whistling was deafening. This was a big night for the Knights. Billy kicked the extra point, and it was 21-0 with only five minutes gone in the first quarter.

It wasn't quite so easy after that. Dalton had called a time-out and that seemed to have settled them down. Dalton was moving the ball slowly but surely, and it looked like they were going in for the score. They ran a sweep to Mickey's side, and he slipped past their lead blocker and hit their back right in the numbers, driving him to the ground. The back quickly jumped to his feet and kicked at Mickey's helmet. Penalty flags were thrown and Billy Brown raced to Mickey's aid.

Mickey was stunned but just stood there and looked at the back. Billy rushed up and grabbed the back, and Mickey thought he was going to hit him. The official was there right away, and then Billy said, "If you can't take a good hit, buddy, you are in the wrong place. Don't they teach you guys better than that?"

The official told Billy to back off, and he did. He grabbed Mickey by the arm, gave him a wink, and said, "Hit him harder the next time. Then he can't get up and kick anyone."

That changed the momentum of the game, and Chad intercepted a pass two plays later, and Fuller went on offense. They kept the ball the remainder of that quarter and three minutes of the second. Both teams exchanged punts, and Fuller had moved the ball to Dalton's eighteen-yard line. In the huddle, Chad said, "Things are getting tougher, so let's show them why we are not going to back down. I just think they are ready for one of you guys to break their back. Let's try an option right on three. Remember, it is on *three*. Ready . . ."

"Break." That sound again. Tubby lined up on the ball, and Chad went through his cadence.

"Ready. Set. Go. Go." No one from Fuller moved, and Dalton's line all rushed. The whistle blew and flags were thrown. A five-yard penalty was assessed, and Fuller had the ball on the thirteen.

Back in the huddle, Chad said, "Same thing, guys. Option right on *four*. Ready . . ."

"Break." Chad started the cadence just like before, but instead Dalton waited. When Chad barked the third go, they came flying across the line again. The whistle blew and penalty flags were thrown. Now they had the ball on the eight-yard line.

Back in the huddle, Chad said, "I'm not sure I can get the signals called without laughing. Those guys must be stinging mad. Okay, now listen. Option right on the first sound. Come off the ball with everything you have. Ready . . ."

"Break." Every player on Fuller's team was smiling, even Chad. He looked right, looked left, and then reached under Tubby and said, "Ready."

Fuller fired off the ball, catching Dalton on their heels. They were expecting another long count but were completely fooled. Chad moved down the line, after faking to Clark, and was ready to pitch to Billy when a Dalton player moved into his pitch line. He planted his right foot, faked a pitch to Billy, and turned toward the goal line. As he turned, he saw Mickey upending the corner, and Chad sprinted into the end zone.

In the huddle for the extra point, Chad looked at his team. They were all smiling. Billy stepped out of the huddle and called time-out. Chad said, "What are you doing?"

"I'll be right back," said Billy. He ran to the sideline and went right to Coach Barron. "Please send someone in for Chad. I'll hold for Mickey. I want Chad to hear the ovation he should have. We get all the glory and he gets none."

Coach Barron just stood there with his mouth open. He turned to Coach Howard and Coach Rowe, and they were doing the same.

168

"Well," Billy said.

The official blew his whistle, and Coach Barron called another time-out. He turned to Billy and said, "In all my years of coaching I have never seen a greater act of kindness than this. You get your wish, Captain." Tears were rolling down Coach Barron's face as he sent Cal Radcliffe into the game with Billy.

When they got to the huddle, Cal Radcliffe yelled, "Anderson out."

Chad looked stunned. The entire crowd looked stunned. No one seemed to know what was going on. Chad looked at Billy, and Billy pointed to the bench. Chad reluctantly headed for the sideline.

As he left the huddle, the crowd on both sides of the field started cheering and whistling. The closer he got to the sideline, the louder it got. When he finally reached the team, they swarmed him. Coach Barron went to him and said, "It is an honor to coach the best quarterback in the state. You make us all look good."

"I don't understand, Coach. It isn't even halftime and you know your rule. No cheering until the last second is off the clock."

"Well, I guess I will just have to run sprints with you on Monday, okay? Enjoy what you deserve."

The final score was 35-7. Following the game, the players were met at the gate by hundreds of people. They had trouble keeping the students off the field. This was big stuff. The principal finally told the faculty to let them have fun but not get destructive.

Mr. Banning and Mickey's dad finally got to him, and Mr. Banning said, "Mickey, this is one of the best high school teams I have ever seen, regardless of class. You played a great game, Son."

"Thanks, Mr. Banning, now we get the playoffs, but this was our goal. All the rest is gravy. It's been a great ride." Just then Sally came running through the crowd and jumped into his arms.

"Ugh! You smell."

"Well, what did you expect?"

"I expected my transfer hero to be immaculate."

"Yeah, right. Dad, take this pretty thing out of my arms. She doesn't like me anymore."

"Yeah, right," she said and jumped back in his arms and kissed him.

"You don't mind, do you, Dad?" she asked her father.

"Heck, no. If he was a girl, I would kiss him myself."

Just then, their two mothers came up, and Mrs. Banning said, "Then I'll do it for you." She grabbed him by the arm and pulled him down and kissed him on the cheek. Mrs. Daniels followed suit.

"Oh, Mickey, you were so wonderful. I wish you guys were still playing, but then I'm not sure my nerves could take it."

"Well, I know you are all going to the malt shop for shakes, so we better let you go get cleaned up because Sally has her eye on someone cleaner," Mr. Daniels said.

"Only on you, Mr. Daniels," and she hugged him and kissed him on the cheek.

"Hey," Mickey started to say.

"Get moving, Son, before I steal your girl."

Mickey grinned and jogged toward the school. Boy did he feel good. All that work and all that sweat was paying off in a big way. He had someone special to celebrate with, too. He quickly showered, gave Gary Pearson a hug, and headed out to Sally's new car, parked right next to Chad's. There she sat, on the top of the seat talking to Brenda and Sue.

"Where did Chad go?" he asked.

"The three captains are talking to the press. They will be out soon, though," Brenda said.

"Okay," said Mickey. "We will save you a seat at the malt shop. I can't wait to see what they say in the papers tomorrow."

They drove away in Sally's car. She let him drive, and he felt like a king. What a lucky man I am!

They headed for the malt shop, and Mickey was thinking about the game. He was so quiet Sally thought something was wrong. She said, "What's wrong, Mickey? Did I say or do something you didn't like?"

"Oh no, not at all. I was just thinking about the game. Wasn't it great the way they cheered for Chad?"

"You aren't going to believe this, but it was Billy who told Coach to take him out so he could be recognized. That was something special. I never thought I would see the day. Look what you have done for this team since you have been here."

"Oh, Sally, it wasn't me. These are all great guys."

"Yes, but Mickey, your presence on the team made everyone more competitive."

"Sally, that isn't you talking. Where did you get all that?"

"Okay, it was my dad. He thinks you have been the spark they needed. You being there made Billy realize what a team can do and that it takes everyone, not just one player. He says by you being in that backfield, they couldn't just key on him and made things tougher for the other team to defense you."

Just then they pulled up to the malt shop. Kids were all over the place. Mickey knew there would be no place for them to sit, but they went in anyway. To his surprise, they had extra tables in the back by the counter, and they were all end to end. Some of the players were already there sitting with their girls. As Mickey and Sally walked up, they all cheered. In unison, they all yelled, "Hurrah! Number 26." Mickey smiled and sat down with Sally. Chad came in and the same thing happened, "Hurrah! Number 4." This continued until they were all there. When Billy came in, the sound was deafening.

Mr. Banning came to their tables and said, "Welcome, Champs!" A roar went up, and he continued, "The Boosters have a little treat." He turned and pointed to the people behind the bar. There were Mrs. Daniels, Mrs. Banning, and Mrs. Anderson.

Mrs. Banning spoke, "I am sure you all know by now that Mrs. Daniels has been feeding Mickey a milk shake every night since he has been in Fuller. We thought you deserved a 'Mrs. Daniels special.'" More hoots and hollers went up. She continued, "This is a great night for our community, and we are proud of all of you as well as the cheerleaders who thought up this idea. We want you to know that we love you all and will be with you throughout the playoffs as you try for the state title." More cheers went up.

Randy said, "Mrs. Banning, are you running for Congress?"

They all laughed, and then Mrs. Daniels said, "Randy, we have a special chair for you over here. Do you recognize it? It's electric."

That really topped it off. Everyone was in a great mood. The cheerleaders started the fight song, and Mickey was sure they could be heard in Dalton. Mickey was thinking about his not wanting to move and now, how happy he was that they did. You couldn't write a better script than this. Sally came to the table with their shakes, and they sat there and smiled at one another. Mickey looked around the shop and saw many kids he didn't know filtering in their group. A stocky little boy about twelve was wearing Randy's jersey. When he came over to the table, Randy got up and said, "Now listen, girls, you be on your best behavior. This is my little brother and I don't want him learning anything he shouldn't."

"You better have him move in with the Coach then," Mrs. Daniels said as she gave him his shake. "He probably is beyond saving already." They all cheered and teased Randy about being one-upped by Mickey's mother.

"I taught him all I know so he can keep all his classmates in line," said Randy.

Again Mrs. Daniels countered with, "How long did that take, five minutes?" Again the place erupted in laughter. Everyone was in a great mood, and Mickey could hardly contain himself.

They all left the shop and headed toward their homes or wherever. When they got back from the shop, they went into Sally's backyard and sat in the two-person swing. He thought about all the things that happened to him since moving to Fuller. There was so much, and there were no negatives. He was happy, and his parents were happy. He sat there with the most wonderful and prettiest girl he knew. Mickey slipped out of the swing and laid down in the grass. Sally looked at him while he was staring at the stars. She joined him and laid her head on one of his arms as he had his hands folded behind his head. She rolled toward him, and they kissed. As she lay back on his arm, he knew he was in heaven, and whatever was to come, he hoped it would be just like this.

"You are my transfer hero, but I'm just glad we are who we are." With that, they just laid there looking at the stars and wondered what they had in store next. They had planned on going to the park on Saturday, win or lose, but Saturday was going to be fun, now.

Mickey got up early and prepared everything they needed for the day. He had a big picnic basket with everything in it. His mother came in the kitchen while he was finishing and told him that many of the parents were going there today, also.

"Mickey, your father and I are going so we will bring the basket. You go get Sally and see what she wants to do about getting there."

"Okay, Mother, I'll go right now. We will see you at the park,"

Mickey put on his sweater and headed out the door. The thought of spending the day with Sally made him feel good. He had no worries. Coach had told them that they were picking all the opponents for the playoffs early on this day, and if he got the info early enough, he would come to the park and tell them who they played the following Saturday. He thought about that, and it made him feel like a college boy playing on a Saturday afternoon.

As he was walking up the sidewalk, Mrs. Banning was coming out the door and met him halfway. "Mickey, you are a little early. You can't go in just yet. Sally has a surprise for you. Come out back and sit on the swing with me for a minute."

The suspense was killing him. He didn't mind, however, because he had a chance to talk to Sally's mother. He said, "I have to tell you, Mrs. Banning, your family is tops. Did Sally tell you what I told her the other day?"

"If you mean that you were falling in love with her. Yes, she did."

"What do you think about that? I sure wouldn't want you and Mr. Banning to think badly of me or anything like that. She is such a great girl."

"Mickey, Mr. Banning and I always let Sally decide things like that for herself. We both are happy a boy like you has finally decided that she is a good person to be with and not a trophy."

"Rest assured, I will not do anything to jeopardize my being able to be with her. Besides, my dad would absolutely kill me."

Sally came out of the house carrying a black sweater. She came over to the swing and motioned for him to stand up, which he was already doing. She was holding a varsity letter sweater with the big block F on the front. She said, "Coach said we could give these to you guys who don't have a letter already. They think it would be neat for all of you to be dressed alike."

Mickey didn't know what to say. He stood there as Sally laid it across his shoulders and said, "Looks like a perfect fit. All the other guys on the team are getting theirs today, instead of waiting for the athletic awards program. Coach thinks the paper will be at the park today."

"Thank you, Sally. Did you sew the letter on?"

"Yep, me and my little sewing fingers."

Mickey yanked his other sweater off and put on the letter sweater. Now, he really was a full-fledged Fuller Black Knight.

174

Sally was grinning from ear to ear. Mrs. Banning gave Mickey a big hug and said, "Looks great on you, Mickey. We will see you at the park in a little while."

Mickey and Sally walked around the house and started down the street. As he passed his house, his mother and dad came out the door. As they walked by, Sally yelled, "How does my transfer hero look now?"

Mickey turned sideways and sported his new sweater and letter. They cheered and waved as Mickey returned the wave and put his arm around Sally. The Daniels were standing there admiring the two of them walking and were elated. "Well, I guess our son is fitting in pretty well," Mr. Daniels said. She gave him a squeeze, and they headed for their car.

When Mickey and Sally got to the park, there were many of the players already there. Billy Brown came up to Mickey and Sally and introduced his girlfriend to them. Billy had a huge grin on his face. Chad came over and said, "Billy, now those people in Dalton will leave you alone."

"Everyone but Sheila. Did you read the paper this morning?"

Mickey had forgotten about the newspaper. All he wanted to know is who they played next Saturday. Just then, Ron Richmond came walking up and said, "Listen, you guys, you have made my week, maybe even my season. That was the greatest game I have ever covered. I could have used the whole sports section."

"Mr. Richmond," Billy said, "I want to thank you for all the nice things you said in the paper today. Comparing us to the Four Horsemen is really an honor."

"Well, many people don't know who they were, but they will get a real history lesson this week. Your Coach is on the way over to tell you who you play on Saturday. Now that is one lucky coach. Most coaches can coach a whole career and never have a team like you."

Coaches Barron, Howard, and Rowe drove in and the team gathered around. There were over a hundred people at the park, and they all came over to the picnic table the coach was standing on.

"We play Hadley on Saturday at one. The best part is we play on an all-weather field at Tobin University. Boys, they are going to see some real speed this Saturday. I can't wait to show off the new version of the Four Horsemen."

They all cheered and started chatting about the next game. "Oh no, you don't, Mr. Hero. You aren't going to talk football for at least three hours," Sally said. She grabbed his hand and walked over to where their parents were sitting on a blanket. Mrs. Banning spread out another blanket for the two of them, and they sat down.

Mr. Banning said, "Mickey, I called the coach at state and told him about Billy and Chad. I also told him there was a junior down here that was just as good. He is seriously thinking about offering Chad and Billy some aid to go to state."

"That would be great. They sure deserve it."

"Well, you do too. You have had a great season. Mickey, I have to tell you, I just can't get over how different it was watching this team this year. Some of the things were pretty awesome."

"Thank you, Mr. Banning."

"Daddy," Sally said, "that is because the transfer hero made it all the more pleasant."

"Well, Coach Barron said that Mickey was the difference in Billy. He just happens to be the missing piece, and now the picture is complete."

Mickey was beside himself. All he really wanted to do was play ball. Everything that happened was like a dream. Sally leaned against him, and her perfume rose into his nostrils. He put his arm around her shoulders and said, "Mr. Banning, I'm in love with your daughter. I . . . ."

"I know, and I'm glad. You two seem to get along pretty good. After that first day, I was wondering what kind of boy would do that to my daughter."

"Gosh, Mr. Banning, I'm really sorry about that. I just . . . ."

"Cut it out and enjoy yourself. That little slap may be the beginning of something big. It sure made Fuller a better team."

Mickey looked at his parents, and they were grinning. Mickey turned and kissed Sally on the cheek and whispered, "You are my inspiration."

She turned quickly and jumped on top of Mickey, holding him to the ground. "If you ever hit me again, transfer hero, you will have to transfer out again."

He held her in his arms so she couldn't hit him anymore. They laughed and played, but Mickey knew that it wouldn't be long before they would be studying film again. Right now, the films could wait. He had all he could handle with the squirming Sally Banning.

The End

9 781462 881307